PRAISE FOR THE GUNS OF LEGENDE

I can't put these suckers down.

— JACKSON LOWRY - WESTERN
FICTIONEER LIFETIME ACHIEVEMENT
AWARD WINNER

Magnificent!

— RICHARD PROSCH - WESTERN WRITERS
OF AMERICA SPUR AWARD WINNER

Brody Weatherford may have written the Great
American Novel.

— THAT GUY WHO'S ALWAYS AT STARBUCKS

D1567893

GOLD FOR GUNS

"Do you have the weapons? I don't see them. I don't even see a wagon loaded with what I'm buying." Frank Landry read the sergeant's uneasiness as worry and not betrayal. "Something's gone wrong? Why don't you have the goods?"

"I can't get the cannons or Gatlings, just the rifles." The sergeant's earlier demeanor had been bravado and nothing more. Frank saw the opening and dug into it.

"And ammunition, bullets and anything else that comes with a brand new Spencer?"

"Look, there's an uprising down around Creede. The whole fort's buzzing about that. The rifles are being loaded onto a wagon right now and will come past in a few minutes. The driver and guards are all my men. You give me the gold and you ride off in the wagon with the goods."

"How many rifles?"

"Fifty."

Frank heard the lie. He waved his hand to show the deal was off. If the sergeant's story about an Indian uprising at Creede was true, the Army and any recruited local militia there needing rifles, he was in a pickle.

THE GUNS OF LEGENDE

YOUR FREE STORY IS WAITING

Delve into the origins of the Guns of Legende and get your FREE bonus copy of a rip-snorting new Western adventure at www.GunsOfLegende.com:

Thunderstick Diplomats

FRONT RANGE REBELLION

The Guns of Legende #1

BRODY WEATHERFORD

The Society of Buckhorn and Bison, Publishers

olonel Carlton Clark settled the Whitfield musket across a small sandbag as he sighted in on the distant lookout. He spread his legs in a vee for stability on the uneven ground and shifted an inch to the right to get away from a rock poking his belly. His finger lightly brushed the trigger, waiting for the precise instant to take out the unsuspecting outlaw.

"You think you can hit him at this range, Colonel? I do declare, it must be eight hundred yards if it's an inch." Harley Blackmun dropped to his knees beside Clark and brushed his elbow enough to jerk the rifle out of proper sighting.

Clark sagged, his concentration broken. He snugged the rifle back into his shoulder and sighted through the Parker-Hale telescopic sight. The cross-hairs once more centered on the far-off man's head, only now the outlaw squatted. Again Clark's shot was ruined. He pulled back and glared at his aide-de-camp.

"What's wrong, Colonel? Did that varmint move?"

"I had a shot for only an instant. I lost my concentration." The implied criticism wasn't understood by Harley Blackmun. Not for the first time, Clark wished he had been able to recruit a better quality second in command. But he, of all people, knew you fought the war with the army you have. If he wasn't able to whip Blackmun into shape, that was as much his fault as the short, stocky, unkempt man's. He was the leader. Blackmun was the lump of clay waiting to be shaped into a proper soldier and fighting man.

"That's a loco looking rifle. I remember seeing some old Brown Bess muskets, but this one's nothing like I ever saw."

"I used it to bring down General Sedgwick at Spotsylvania." Clark once more drew the stock in to his shoulder and peered through the telescopic sight.

"I've seen my share of Winchesters and other rifles. .44 and .45 and other calibers. What one's this?"

"It's a .451." Clark had no time to discuss arms or munitions. The train robbery was close to being a reality. "Have our scouts pinpointed the other outlaws?"

"Last I heard from Willie, he found eight of them. They've got dynamite planted in the notch at the top of the pass. When the train comes chugging uphill, all slowed down and straining to make the grade, they'll set it off and maybe derail the engine."

"We must stop them escaping if we fail to reach them quickly," the colonel said. "What of their horses?"

"Willie and that Ute he calls a blood brother found a rope corral just over the pass. Give the word, and we steal their horses."

Colonel Clark took out an elaborate timepiece, opened the cover and peered at the face as if memorizing every numeral. He snapped it shut finally and replaced it in his side jacket pocket.

"Take their horses now. The train will be here before we know it." He pressed his eye back into the end of the telescopic sight. A quick blink let him focus once more on his

outlaw target. Clark's breath caught for a moment in anticipation. The outlaw stood and took off his hat, ready to wave
it to signal the rest of the gang.

Clark exhaled and waited for his heart beat to settle. It
was now or never. His finger drew back on the musket trigger.
The sharp recoil surprised him. Good. He hadn't flinched in
anticipation. A quick look through the scope brought a tiny
smile to his lips. His bullet knocked the train robber off his
perch. The outlaw was dead before the report from the rifle
ever reached the spot where he had stood lookout.

"Glory be, Colonel. That's one fine shot."

"Now, Captain Blackmun, get our company moving. We
still have one hellacious fight ahead of us." Clark sat cross
legged and began tending his precious Whitfield. He
removed the telescopic sight and wrapped it in oilcloth. The
rifle itself was returned to a padded case. It should never be
thrust into a saddle sheath where brush might scratch its
highly polished stock or damage the metal.

He worked methodically to store the weapon. Even when
he heard distant gunfire, he refused to hurry. Only when he
secured the Whitfield did he stand and stretch cramped
muscles. He wasn't as young as he once was. A quick shrug of
his shoulders settled his olive-drab officer's jacket with its
intentionally dulled gold braid. The brass buttons had similarly been purposefully tarnished to camouflage him during
the coming battle. He preferred the brilliance of a full-dress
uniform, with shining gold braid and brass buttons reflecting
so much light that they caused the unwary to squint. But that
was for formal conditions, not the battlefield.

In spite of thinning silver hair and a face wrinkled like a wind-
blown desert sand dune, his ramrod straight military bearing
made him look far younger than his sixty years. At six feet he
towered above the others crowding around him, intent to hear
his orders. A lifetime of battles, both in the United States and in

Central America had taken their toll on him, however. His left knee locked on occasion and shrapnel in his right thigh reminded him of lost campaigns in both Costa Rica and Nicaragua.

This fight would be different. He had right on his side now.

He carefully placed his rifle into a crevice for later retrieval. For now, it was safe from scratches, and there wasn't any moisture on the rock to damage the precious musket. A step back and a look around fixed the hiding place in his mind.

It was time to get on with the mission. He made his way down the slope to the railroad tracks where Blackmun had assembled the troops. They were a scruffy looking bunch of scoundrels. For now, that suited him. Later, more military discipline would be required when they took to the field for the battles to come.

"Gentlemen, you have been drilled so that each knows his proper role." He studied the dozen men. Some shuffled about nervously, but most of them had taken part in train robberies before and knew what to expect. Those were the soldiers he depended on most at the moment. The others would learn.

Or die.

"Yeah," cut in Blackmun, "you spotted that scout real good. The colonel here took him out with a single shot from up there." Harley Blackmun puffed up as if he had been the sniper. "He dropped that varmint from eight hundred yards like he was a buffalo." He cleared his throat and spoke even louder, "Eight hundred yards is one hell of a shot."

"We all have our skill, our duty," Colonel Clark cut in, regaining the attention of his men. "The outlaws are trying to snake us out of our due. Don't let them. I expect you to defend yourselves in the performance of our mission." He stood just a tad taller and struck a pose, hand over his heart.

"This is for God and country. Our new country. Don't let a one of them get the drop on you or climb on top of that train to seize the high ground."

Silence fell over the men gathered along the railroad tracks. Clark studied each in turn with his iron-gray eyes.

"For our country!"

This time a cheer went up. Colonel Clark waved them out to the battle. Blackmun shooed the men to specific places, but the narrow, rocky gap funneled them toward the slope. Clark stepped onto the nearest rail and put his weight down. Vibration told him the train wasn't far away as it struggled up the steep slope.

He drew his .44-40 Colt Peacemaker, cocked it and started forward. As he marched toward the gap, shots echoed all around him. His men removed the outlaws who had the mettle to attempt the train robbery. Clark was certain none of the owlhoots would be left to stand trial. Such judicial proceedings would only be a waste of time. Better to take care of them at the scene of their crime.

"Lookee there, Colonel. See? Up high." Blackmun tugged his sleeve and pointed into the rocks. "You nailed him smack in the middle of his head. That was one fine shot. I can believe you took out that Federal general back in the day just like you said."

Before Clark could stop the gushing praise, the ground shook. His weakened legs caused him to stumble. He used Blackmun as a prop to keep from falling until he regained his balance. Ahead an avalanched slid down the mountain and dumped large boulders across the tracks.

"Our troopers failed to stop the blaster," Clark said in disgust. "Now we have to climb over the rocks to reach the train." Worse, he fumed, this meant the train robbers were in position to board the train. "Send a few men uphill to get rid of whoever set the explosives. Don't let them linger. We will need every gun aboard the train."

Blackmun dashed off, shouting orders as he went. Clark shook his head sadly. It was so hard to recruit competent officers. He climbed over piles of gravel scattered across the railroad tracks, then reached the spot where boulders blocked the iron rails. Gunshots greeted him as he rounded the miniature mountain.

The train had been able to stop before plowing into the stony barricade. The engineer was draped over the window in the cab. His striped had fallen to the ground and blood from a head wound dripped onto it. Clark made his way to the step into the cab. He gripped the handhold with his left hand and pointed his Peacemaker with the other as he pulled himself up. The stoker sprawled across the coal. He had taken a pair of slugs in the chest. Clark went to the engineer's controls and looked them over. He vented a long, loud whistle, then found the valve that dumped the steam in the boiler. If it ran dry, the engine would turn into an iron brick, useless, never again to roll from the western slopes across the Front Range into Denver with its cargo of gold from a dozen mines from Victor all the way north to Central City.

More gunfire rang out. He lowered himself gingerly, favoring his aching legs, then ran as fast as he could to the first passenger car. A quick look inside showed the robbers had massacred a half dozen passengers. A tiny smile crept to his thin lips when he saw one bandit had met his maker. He had confronted a passenger who had used a derringer on him to good effect. But the defense had been in vain. The passenger had been drilled clean through the heart, possibly at the same instant he had fired his toy of a pistol.

Clark continued along the train, heading for the sounds of gunfire farther back. Two of his soldiers were pinned down by a bandit in the third passenger car.

"Attack," Clark bellowed. "Don't let the enemy cow you!"

"But, Colonel, they got rifles and hostages."

Clark made a note of the soldier who complained about doing his duty. There would be time to deal with him afterward, after the action. He snatched the man's six-shooter from his hand, then walked to the iron platform between cars. His legs felt good. Once more he was in combat. With his shoulder, he slammed open the door into the car.

"You stay back!" An outlaw at the other end of the Pullman waved his six-gun around, then he put it to a woman's head.

"Don't let him kill me, mister. Please. I've got--"

Clark took aim and fired. His bullet tore through the woman's midriff and embedded in the outlaw's breadbasket. The robber staggered back a step. Clark's next two shots dispatched him. He made his way down the aisle, looking left and right. The outlaws had killed everyone else in the car. He stopped to look down at the woman. She clutched her stomach. Red blossoming around her fingers told the tale.

"Y-you shot me," she said in a voice so weak it was barely a whisper.

"It was the outlaw's fault, ma'am. Take comfort in knowing that he is dead."

Clark saw that the woman was dead, also. He stepped over her and went to the door from the car and opened it. The freight car was next in the train. The door leading into where mail and other valuables were transported was securely bolted. Beyond that barrier lay the gold being shipped to Denver banks. He emptied one six-shooter into the door and only sent a few splinters flying. Not a single hunk of lead tore through the thick, seasoned wood. With a quick, sure movement, he thrust the empty pistol into his belt.

He dropped to the ground and saw that his men worked to force open the freight car door. He left them to their chore and hurried to the caboose. Streaks of light reflected in the narrow upper windows as a gunfight raged inside. Clark rounded the back of the caboose and climbed onto the rear platform. A few turns on the brake set it securely enough to keep the train from running away downhill should the caboose disconnect from the rest of the train.

The back door exploded open and a man wearing the striped hat of a crewman half fell from inside. He looked up and saw Clark's uniform.

"There're robbers in there. Held up the train. Stop them."

Clark turned his gun on the man and killed him with a single shot to the head. Red began staining the black and white stripes on his hat. Stepping over the body and entering the caboose cautiously, Clark looked around. Bunks on either side provided a place for the train crew to sleep while the train was rolling from one station to the next. He edged forward, then turned and fired three times into a lump of blanket on a lower bunk. A loud cry of pain rewarded his attention to detail. Blankets did not stir about on their own.

A quick yank pulled the covering to the floor. An outlaw curled up in a tight ball. Clark looked at him dispassionately and fired the last of his rounds. The man stopped writing about.

"Hold your fire!" Clark called out as the door at the other end of the caboose opened a crack. Without hurrying, he reloaded his Peacemaker. "Are the rest of the outlaws dead?"

The door opened halfway and a man timidly glanced past the edge. Seeing his colonel, he pushed the door open all the way.

"We cut down the lot of 'em. The only ones left are in the freight car."

Clark snorted at such illogic. He motioned for the man to jump to the ground.

"The outlaws couldn't get into the gold. They didn't have

time. We were too effective in stopping them." He felt as if he explained the situation to a small child. Only railroad guards were left. No matter their past crimes against men trying to ride the rails, they weren't train robbers.

Clark followed his soldier to the freight car. The men working on the door had pried loose part of the track where the tall wood panel rolled shut.

"We should have brung dynamite," Harley Blackmun said. "I wanted to. We can go see if they had any left after they brought down half the damned mountainside to block the train." He started to send a couple men to hunt.

"They used it all," Clark snapped. "Keep the men together in a squad. If you scatter them all over the battlefield, they can be picked off one by one."

"But we killed everybody. Even the passengers," Blackmun protested.

Clark examined the door track, slid his fingers under it and yanked hard. The metal bent with a loud groan. He continued to pull until it fell free. When it did, the door had no lower support. It came loose from the upper track and fell outward.

The instant it did, Clark and his men opened fire on the three men inside the car. The clerk and two guards died under the fusillade. He waved Blackmun and another inside. They started rummaging through the mail bags. He worried that Blackmun wasn't able to read well enough, but they hunted for official letters being sent to the territorial gover-nor. All they had to look for was an official seal on an envelope.

As they scattered mail around the car, Clark pulled himself up and went to the safe. He fished around in a coat pocket and found a slip of paper. Using it as his guide, he dialed in the combination. The safe opened on his second try.

He tossed aside the scrap of paper and basked in the golden radiance pouring from the safe.

"Take it out, men," he ordered. He stepped away and let his soldiers drag the gold bars from the safe. He inventoried them as they carried the gold to the door. Ten bars of bullion, each weighing close to twenty-five pounds each. Four thousand ounces. He nodded in satisfaction. His cause just received an involuntary donation of $75,000.

"They're bringing the horses around, Colonel," Blackmun called to him. "But we got other trouble brewing."

He tilted his head to one side and listened. Gunfire from the passenger cars reached him. He almost blurted out what he thought of Blackmun not dealing with this himself, then he swallowed his criticism. With the gold, attracting better qualified officers would be possible. First arms, then trained officers.

Then, *then*!

"You want to do something about them, Colonel?"

"Captain Blackmun, tend to the gold. See that it is properly stored." An approaching rider led a magnificent black stallion. Clark whistled. Bucephalus reared, forcing the man with the reins to drop them. The horse pawed the air before trotting to him.

Clark stepped out of the freight car and settled into the saddle. He wheeled the stallion about and walked forward, leering in the passenger car windows as he went. In the second car he saw the conductor clutching a six-shooter. Two of his men had been wounded and had taken refuge behind seats.

He hopped from horseback to the forward platform. For a moment he steadied himself, then kicked open the door. The conductor spun and started to fire. The uniform stayed his hand.

"You done come jist in time. There's two robbers in the back of this here car."

Clark pressed his index finger to his lips. He walked the length of the car until he found his two cowering soldiers.

"You men are a disgrace," he said.

"You get him, Colonel? Did you--" The man got no farther. Clark dispatched him with a single shot and turned to the second of the incompetents.

"Why'd you go and do that, Colonel?" The man came close to blubbering. "Me and Joshua got ambushed by the conductor. We didn't think he'd have a gun."

"No, you didn't think. What you did was show incompetence. Perhaps that is my fault for not providing adequate training. You both also revealed a deep streak of cowardice. I will not tolerate that." Another shot ended the man's life. He heard footsteps behind and turned. The conductor used the seats for support as he came back, trailing blood. He had been shot in the thigh.

"You didn't try to arrest them. What kind of lawman are you?"

Clark said, "No kind at all." Then he shot the conductor. His aim was far better than that of his two dead soldiers.

"We got the horses all loaded up," called Blackmun from alongside the train. "You need any help, Colonel?"

Clark reached in his pocket and found a printed piece of paper the size of a playing card.

"None required, Captain. You hightail it. I must retrieve my rifle before joining you."

He looked at the card, then tossed it onto the conductor's dead body.

It read: Free Nation of Auraria.

2

That'll be two cents," Augustus Crane said, hefting the envelope handed him by the bespectacled man.

"That's an outrage! Two cents! We won't pay that much when we become a state." The postal customer sputtered and looked as if he wanted to snatch the envelope from Crane's hand.

Gus moved a little back from the counter to prevent that. He was feeling cantankerous today and bedeviled the shop-keeper for no good reason. His gnarled fingers stroked over the envelope, and he lifted the missive to sniff daintily. His bulbous nose quivered at the scent of violet toilet water. The thick dark mustache, shot with gray, twitched and his bushy eyebrows wriggled like wooly caterpillars. Sharp blue eyes fixed on the man.

"Postage due is postage due. It's my duty as postmaster for the great city of Denver. And it won't change one iota when we become a state. I am duly appointed by the Post-master of the United States to this post."

"You liar," the man snapped. "You paid a bribe for it. All you government employees did."

"You're angry because you were passed over when I was appointed last year," Gus said, beginning to enjoy the exchange. "You'll be even angrier if you don't pay the postage due. The lady that wrote this is either clumsy with her perfume or thinks the world of you."

"What do you mean?" The shopkeeper pressed against the far side of the counter and prepared to grab. Gus moved back another half step.

"The amount of sweet smellum soaking this letter tells me she either knocked over a perfume bottle, which is quite likely, seeing what a testy fellow you are, or she wanted to drop enough on so it arrived to ... entice you."

"Here. Take your filthy ransom money." The man dropped two pennies on the counter with ill grace. "I suppose you'll tell me you read the letter."

"I'd never do such a thing. I have scruples and uphold my oath to the Constitution." Gus held out the letter for the man to snatch away. "Which is why you didn't get the job and I did."

"What's that? Eh?" The man squinted as he peered over his spectacles.

"I'd never have thought of reading mail not addressed to me. You, on the other hand, thought of it instantly, showing that you'd do it." Gus made shooing motions with his bony hand. "Go on, get away. I have other customers."

The man looked over his shoulder. They were alone in the post office lobby. He started to argue, then clutched the letter to his breast and left, mumbling curses as he went. Gus waited for him to vanish from the Capitol Hill Post Office before taking a sealed courier pouch from under the counter. He stared at it. No imprint showed that this contained official US Mail. He knew no postage had been paid on the contents because none was needed when his chief in Washington, D.C. sent orders--and he knew whoever gave the terse orders was not the Postmaster General. He had his suspicions but never asked.

He never even made discreet inquiries with highly placed officials back in the nation's Capitol, and in a short time to be Colorado's, too.

Rather than open the leather laces securing the pouch, he ran his fingers around the edge until he found a protruding tiny metal spike. He looked out onto Marion Street to be sure no new annoying customers would divert him, then bent the spike to one side. The bottom seam opened an inch, just wide enough for him to fish about inside. If he had opened the pouch in a normal fashion this hidden pocket would never have been revealed. Only worthless encoded letters would tumble out. By the time anyone intercepting the pouch gave up trying to read the letters or, as Gus suspected, deciphered the code and was sent on a wild goose chase, the real information would have become outdated and useless.

His unknown commander never gave assignments that weren't to be done quickly, sometimes with seemingly impossible deadlines.

He twisted the single sheet around his finger and slowly drew it out. The white paper was nondescript. No betraying watermark, no hint as to where it had been bought or whose office had sent it. The precise, even script written in gray ink was as much a verification of its authenticity as the method of delivery. Gus had seen enough orders written in that hand to pay special attention.

Reading through it twice caused him to suck in his breath and hold it until his lungs began to ache. He had to force himself to breathe. Too many missions assigned him seemed trivial, even if they ended up with significant outcomes. This one, though, screamed of immediate danger.

He pressed his finger down next to a single name at the bottom: Rafe Fenstermacher.

Gus tossed the pouch back under the counter, fumbled in his pocket and found a tin of lucifers. A quick movement ignited the match. The paper with the gray ink writing burned completely in seconds. He made a face when he suffered a small burn on his arthritic fingers. It was enough to assure him that only ash remained.

He turned toward the rear of the post office and bellowed, "Bernard, fetch me a package for Rafe Fenstermacher. And do it now. None of your lollygagging!"

The clerk scurried out like a rat from a sinking ship. He was three inches shorter than Augustus Crane's five-foot-nine and stocky compared to his boss' thin to the point of emaciation build. He held the package in both hands, as if offering a sacrifice to the gods of Olympus. Bernard's rheumy eyes held Gus' gimlet stare for an instant before he looked away, as if he was nothing more than a schoolboy caught passing notes in class.

"Anything else you want, Mister Crane? This musta just come in. Don't know anybody named this."

"I'll personally deliver it." Gus took the package. It was light as a feather and made almost no sound as he rocked it to and fro. Whatever was inside amounted to only a few sheets of paper, although the box was large enough to hold a six-shooter.

"You sure do know a lot people, Mister Crane. And they all have odd names."

"This is the first package I've delivered in a month or more," Gus said, not wanting to dally. Getting into a long conversation with the assistant postmaster wasn't anything he desired, either. Bernard seemed a dullard, but Gus knew more went on in that domed skull than any casual acquaintance might realize. Bernard read dime novels and imagined vast tides of conspiracy and gunplay swirling all around, unseen but there if only he paid close enough attention.

His fiction was just that, fiction. Gus smiled ruefully. If Bernard only knew about the real dangers--the ones countered by a mysterious man in Washington and those in his employ. First came the letter, usually containing a name to match on a package. Gus wondered how many unclaimed parcels he had on post office shelves in the backroom were decoys or details for missions never assigned. The names were peculiar to keep from accidentally giving the package out.

It would never do to have the wrong John Jones or Mary Smith pick up a special package.

He set the package on the edge of the counter, slipped off his canvas apron with its voluminous pockets, then shrugged into his coat. He settled his hat squarely on his head and picked up the package.

"Get on back to your sorting, Bernard. I'll return in two shakes of a lamb's tail."

"Two shakes," Bernard grumbled. "That's one slow shaking sheep, if you ask me. Last time you said that, you were gone for half a day."

"You're in charge. Do your duty, sir!"

Bernard, buoyed somewhat by the vote of confidence, returned to the back room. Gus reached under the counter and found his Smith & Wesson .38. It slid into his leather-lined coat pocket. He was quicker on the draw from that pocket, lined to be certain the pistol hammer never caught in fabric, than many a gunman. He knew. He had shot more than his share in his day.

Prepared, Augustus Crane left with the package securely tucked under his arm. If luck favored him, the recipient would be at home. Otherwise, tracking him down was always quite the chore.

Crane stood in the street outside the three-story house and studied the Victorian Slick style architecture. The house was well maintained, with a cupola that, Crane saw after careful study, contained a telescope for study of the surrounding buildings. The walls were typical, but here and there metal sheeting poked out, hinting that the building was more fortress than home.

A hand-carved sign dangled over the steps leading to the porch proclaimed this as the headquarters for the Society of Buckhorn and Bison. Crane had never pressed the house's occupant, Allister Legende, about that. He didn't really care if this was a meeting place for Elk or Moose or Masons or, whatever they might be, Buckhorns and Bisons. All that mattered was Legende's stellar record at solving problems sent by ... Washington.

Crane opened the iron gate and marched up the flagstone path. A few of the stones needed to be reset. That was unusual for Legende to overlook such simple maintenance. It made Crane want to examine the flagstones more carefully to see what had been buried beneath them. Then it occurred to him that he might not want to do such a foolish thing. He looked up at the windows and metal-backed siding. To go along with such defenses might be land mines buried under the walkway.

He stepped along faster, slowing only when he reached the steps. His knees protested, cracking with each step until he reached the porch and faced the hand-carved double mahogany doors decorated with lead crystal and elaborately patterned stained glass. Crane made out a buckhorn rampant on one door and a bison head on the other. To one side was a door pull. He gave it a yank and stepped back. The wait was only a few seconds. As he suspected, a lookout had alerted the butler of an approaching visitor long before he mounted the front steps.

"Mister Crane," the liveried servant said. Crane saw a telltale bulge under the man's left arm. The only question was how large a caliber pistol was holstered in the shoulder rig.

"Mister Kingston." Crane bent slightly in a bow.

"Please, sir, just Kingston."

"I have a package for Mister Legende."

Kingston waited for the postmaster to hand it over. When he didn't, the butler stepped back to let Crane enter.

"Mister Legende will meet you in the library. This way, sir." Kingston strode off, chin high as if he were the master of the mansion. Crane wondered which army claimed the butler as their own. The slight accent hinted that it might not be an American regiment. Like everything else around Allister Legende, the butler's history was shrouded in mystery.

Mostly, Crane didn't care as long as Legende continued to get the desired results, but curiosity did tug at his sleeve now and then. He slipped past Kingston as he went into the library. A quick look around showed only two scroll wingback chairs on either side of a white marble top table. The chairs were placed near the bay window, giving ample light for easy reading. When the velvet curtains were drawn, a kerosene lamp on the table provided illumination.

Crane walked over and looked at the book on the table. He suspected Legende had been reading it since a bright red grosgrain ribbon marked a page a quarter of the way through. He tried to read the faded embossed gilt title, but his eyesight wasn't up to it.

"*Vom Kriege*," came a booming baritone. "Have you read Clausewitz?"

"Not in the original German," Crane said. He turned. His mouth opened, but he cut off the question. He knew the single door from the library into the outer hall had not opened. The reflection in the glass window had not shifted one iota.

He looked around and wondered where another door, a

hidden one, opened. It had to move a section of the floor to ceiling bookcases, in spite of how heavy a load that meant for hinges due to the shelved books.

Allister Legende silently pointed to one of the wingback chairs. Crane considered how Legende would react if he sat in the other. From the wear marks, Legende spent far more time in the right-hand chair than the one he indicated for Crane. Such a silent battle of wills accomplished nothing and might prejudice Legende accepting the mission.

Crane sank down gratefully. His knees weren't up for long distances, even though the walk from the post office wasn't that far. He laid the package with the bogus name on the marble-topped table.

Legende moved like a ghost, gliding rather than walking. He was tall, easily six feet three, and well muscled but not stocky. Crane thought of a lanky cowboy riding the range rather than the ranch owner. Muscle and steel wire rather than bulging belly and slight waddle in his walk. Cold gray eyes fixed on Crane. Crane had not wanted a battle of wills, but here it was. Legende challenged him. Crane felt outgunned in many ways since he invaded Legende's territory.

Legende wore a fancy smoking jacket with a starched white shirt beneath billowing out ruffles. His trousers likely cost more than Crane made in six months in his job as postmaster. If Crane hadn't looked the other man in the eye, he would have been dazzled by the brilliant sheen from expensive leather shoes.

"Would you care for some refreshment?" Legende sounded sincere. Crane considered the hike back to the post office and decided a few minutes more would not be amiss.

"You have an excellent cellar. Some of that wine you served the last time I was here would hit the spot."

Legende pursed his lips, then said, "I expected you to ask for more of the bourbon, but that was several months ago.

Let me think." Even as he spoke, he reached over and rang a bell behind the kerosene lamp on the table.

Kingston entered, carrying a silver salver with two wine glasses. The red wine had already been poured.

"Thank you, Kingston." Legende lifted his glass and peered through it. "A St Emilion Bordeaux. King Edward enjoyed it. Why shouldn't we?" Legende raised his glass in a toast.

Crane didn't bother sniffing the wine or genteelly sampling it. He knocked it back, rolled it around in his mouth, then swallowed. He placed the drained crystal wine glass on the table. Kingston made it disappear as if by magic.

"As good as before, sir. I must get back to work." He glanced at the box. "I trust you will take this assignment."

"Have you examined what's in the box?"

"Do you mean have I read the details?" Crane shook his head. "From many sources, I suspect I already know what's being asked of you."

Legende tented his fingers and looked at Crane over the tips. He pursed his thin lips and nodded slowly.

"While your sources are more widespread, and higher placed, I believe we are both right guessing what's inclosed." Legende reached out and touched the box with his fingertips. Then he stood and thrust out his hand. "A good day to you, sir."

Crane levered himself to his feet, then shook Legende's hand.

"And to you, sir. I hope you've learned a great deal from your reading." He tapped the book. With that he left, Kingston opening the door for him for the hike back to the post office.

3

F rank Landry stood in the doorway, the swinging saloon doors held wide. He cut a handsome figure and knew it. This time of the day there were only three dance hall girls in the Oak Bucket. They worked the customers they had until they caught sight of him. Tall, well built, a trim mustache and beard so blond it was almost white, he cast his gaze around the room, lingering a moment on each of the young ladies before moving on. His blue eyes stopped on the barkeep, a man of indeterminate age, hair and eyes ordinary in all respects and with a furtive look that made him seem about ready to cut and run because of some unknowable indiscretion.

Frank settled his expensive frock coat and smoothed the paisley vest, lingering a moment to trace the gold watch in a pocket. His nimble fingers slipped down the chain and pressed into a fob, a four-leaf clover imprisoned between two slivers of clear glass crystal. The lucky piece always served him well, except when it came to dealing with the woman who had given it to him. If anything she had drained his luck with this, but he had spent three years regaining it. For the past year it had never failed him.

From the expressions of everyone in the room, it wouldn't fail him now.

He strode forward, boots making a steady click against the floorboards. This was one thing he liked about Denver saloons. They were prosperous enough to have something beneath the sawdust other than a dirt floor. During the past month he had been in too many gin mills that never even bothered to sweep away the sawdust and replace it with fresh. After being in such down on their luck cesspools, clumps of blood-clotted wood pulp stuck to his fine boots like glue. It always took special work to clean them since he seldom trusted the chore to urchins all begging to do the work for a dime.

With a heave, Frank lifted a leather case to the bar and began unfastening the straps. He stopped when one of the soiled doves came over and pressed close.

"I ain't seen you in here before. You new in town?"

"No, but you are, my sweet." He flashed a winning smile. Her breasts rose and fell under her thin dress a little faster at the attention.

"I've worked here for nigh on a month, and I never seen you here." She laid a hand flat on his chest, testing his heartbeat. A puzzled look crossed her face when it didn't speed up at her touch. It pounded out a steady, regular beat.

"I visit this fine establishment every other month. Isn't that right, Joseph?"

The barkeep muttered and started to move to the far end of the bar.

"Don't go running off. We've got business to discuss."

"Why not me and you do the discussin'? Upstairs?" the woman asked. She stroked his arm. He pulled away from her naked insistence. His jacket opened enough to reveal the Colt

Navy slung low in a cross-draw holster on his left hip. She backed off. "There's no need to get testy, mister. We can have fun without you usin' that smoke wagon."

"Joseph and I will conduct our business, then perhaps we can talk." Frank rested his hand on the ebony butt of the six-shooter. Originally a cap and ball, he had paid good money to an expert gunsmith to refit it for .36 cartridges. The balance was still perfect, the aim true and the bullet erupted from the hexagonal barrel reliably on target every time he fired. If faced with the choice, Frank Landry would have walked down Larimer Street buck naked as long as he got to keep his six-gun.

"You know him, Joe?" the woman asked nervously, not wanting any part of a gunfight.

"Trust me, Joseph knows me. And I trusted him. That's what makes me sad. No, more than that. I am disappointed, Joseph, I really am. You've failed to get me the five-hundred dollars you owe me. Now how can I possibly sell you this fine collection of popskull and rotgut on credit when you've shown how unreliable you are paying your debts?"

"Frank, it's been slow. The old Oak Bucket's leaking like a sieve, and I mean money, not water. I meant to send you your money. I did, but there's hardly enough revenue to keep the place open."

"It's more than a simple traveling whiskey peddler you're cheating, Joseph. My employer back in Kansas City expected that money. The money helps pay off transport charges on river barges coming down the Ohio from the Kentucky distilleries. This means you're not only trying to renege on paying me but the Mudflats Distribution Company, some unnamed riverboat captain, *and* the distiller. I won't even mention railroads and freighters bringing in my fine product for you to sell. Why, Joseph, you seem intent on owing money to everyone in these United States."

"We ain't a state yet. Not for a spell and maybe not then. I heard tell that—"

"I'm not the sort to hold a grudge." Frank hardly seemed to move, but the Colt Navy left his holster, cocked and settled on the bar. The muzzle pointed at the shifty-eyed bartender. "Never let it be said that Frank Landry wasn't there to listen to a man's tale of woe without showing a hint of human compassion." He rested his finger on the trigger and adjusted the aim to follow the nervous bartender as he backed away.

"You can't get blood out of a rock, Frank. I don't have it."

"Ladies, how's business been the past couple months?" Frank's booming voice filled the nearly empty saloon.

The women stayed quiet, but one of the customers piped up. "I just blowed in from Georgetown out in Clear Creek County a week back. This place has been booming ever mother lovin' time I've been in, and that's been plenty 'cuz I want to see my Dolly." He tried to kiss the woman to his right. She avoided his wet smooch. That didn't seem to bother him none. "Never seen it empty after eight or nine o'clock any night of the week. On Saturday when they got that purty little singer from San Francisco up on stage, the crowd's packed in like sardines."

"And do these little fishies spend their hard earned money when they're here?" Frank smiled. Joseph turned pale.

"I heard him braggin' how they have to carry the money out in wheelbarrows."

"Sir, you are one fine gentleman. Have a bottle of Billy Taylor's finest as your reward. Compliments of the Mudflats Distribution Company." He never took his eyes off the barkeep as he reached into his case and pulled out a full bottle of whiskey. A quick move sent it sliding down the bar. The soiled dove intercepted it and held the fifth in both hands as if afraid it might escape.

"Help him with that bottle, why don't you, my dear? You'll both agree that you've never let smoother bourbon whiskey slither down your gullet."

"Frank, you--" Joseph reached under the bar. The whiskey salesman moved to put the case between him and the barkeep. He rested the Colt on top of the case.

"Go on, Joseph. Pick a bottle. Any that catches your eye. Make it a flashy label or a brand you don't have on the back bar. I want you to try it out. Your customers deserve the best, and how are they to expect that if the owner and manager doesn't sample what he sells?"

"Frank, you don't have to--"

The only muscle Frank moved was his trigger finger. The six-gun exploded and sent a bullet along the top of the barkeep's skull. It parted his greasy hair and left a smoking track without breaking skin.

"Try some, Joe. Now."

"What you got in there?" Joseph stood on tiptoe and peered into the case. He reached for a bottle, then stopped, looking up. Frank motioned for him to take out the bottle. The barkeep looked at it, then hefted it. "This stuff any good?"

"Take a swig. Take two." Frank kept the six-shooter trained on the man. When he hesitated, Frank said, "I insist."

Little by little Joseph downed the bottle. Halfway he was still going strong, but by the time only a couple fingers remained in the bottle, he was hardly able to stand up. The women whispered among themselves and the men with them laughed aloud at how drunk the barkeep was. They began wagering how long before he passed out.

"Now, sir, your bill to my company is five hundred dollars. With the two cases of this fine liquor you're ordering right now, that's another two hundred. Fork over seven hundred.

Gold if you've got it, greenbacks if you don't. I'm not taking any IOUs today."

"T-too much. D-d-don't have it."

"Keep drinking. You've got a couple ounces left."

"Gonna puke from so much."

"I'll add an ounce of lead to it if you do." Frank watched him turn a little green around the gills. Joseph might have been drunker than a skunk but he heard the truth in the whiskey peddler's words. "Or you might pay me what you owe. Then I'll let you get right on back to spitting on your glasses to polish them."

"What? He does that!" One of the customers knocked over his chair as he tried to stand. The women on either side pulled him down and both whispered in a different ear to settle him down a mite. Grumbling, he righted his chair and let the soiled doves stroke his stubbled chin and tell him how brave he was.

"The money," Frank repeated. "Do you want me to come around the bar and hunt for it myself? I get confused if I'm on that side and can't count too well."

"Steal my money? You cain't do that. That's ... that's stealin'."

"Call it an advance on a bigger shipment of fine rye whiskey. Or you can pay me my due. There wouldn't be any question how much you gave me then."

Joseph fell to the floor. Frank leaned over and watched him crawl on hands and knees to the end of the bar. It took five tries before he opened a small combination safe. He took out a sack of coins and sat, propped against a cabinet. Counting proved as hard for him as standing, but he finally got the twenty dollar gold pieces clutched in his hand. With great determination, he stood and staggered back.

Frank planted both feet on the floor and waited for Joseph

to fork over the money. When the barkeep finished, Frank pushed one double eagle back, saying, "You gave me too much. I don't work for tips. Thank you kindly. Here." He dropped the coins into a vest pocket and shoved a sheet of paper across.

"Wassit?"

"Your receipt. Everything's by the book. Now let me help you earn a profit on some of that money."

Frank closed the case and took the whiskey bottle with the few ounces remaining and joined the ladies and their customers. He set the bottle in the middle of the table, then pulled up a chair.

"Gents, ladies, you are about to experience the finest whiskey this side of the Big Muddy." He poured shots all around, including one for himself.

He held it aloft in a toast and said, "To the Oak Bucket, where only the finest whiskey is served!" Frank knocked it back and appreciated the way it slid down his gullet and pooled warmly in his belly. He wasn't lying when it came to praising his product. The Mudflats Company booze was the best, and he'd drink to that any day of the week and twice on Sundays, blue laws permitting.

"There's not enough for another round," one of the women complained. "Are you buying?" She planted a tiny kiss on Frank's cheek.

"Joseph is so pleased to be serving this fine drink, he'll declare it to be on the house." Frank saw that Joseph was close to passing out from being forced to drink so much whiskey so fast.

The woman laughed, looked at Frank's case. A shake of his head sent her behind the bar to find whatever he had sold Joseph before. She returned and put the bottle down.

"To a night of drinking the good stuff!" she cried.

The others at the table started to cheer. When they fell

ominously silent, Frank half turned and rested his hand on his six-gun.

Then he was lifted bodily and held at arm's length by the biggest, meanest looking thug he had ever seen.

"Come with me," the mountain of gristle and mean said.

"If I don't want to?" Frank's teeth rattled as the giant shook him like a terrier with a rat clamped in its jaws. "All right, you've convinced me. Put me down."

He was lowered. As his boots touched the floor, he went for his Colt. His arm refused to budge. A meaty hand circled his wrist and held him as if he were a small child.

"Sorry," Frank said insincerely." The pressure on his wrist eased. "I meant to ask with whom I have the pleasure of leaving this fine drinking emporium. And where are we heading?"

"I'm Mister Small."

"Of course you are," Frank said uneasily. "And where did you say we were going?"

"I didn't." The powerful hand seized Frank's collar and pulled him along. Frank started to protest about leaving his sample case behind, but Mister Small carried it in his other hand without showing a hint of strain.

Frank Landry wished he had matched Joseph drink for drink. This kidnaping might have been more tolerable then.

❧ 4 ❧

Emily O'Connor laughed at the poor joke and used her fan to hide her mouth from the attorney general. She batted her long eyelashes at the man who was older than dirt but obviously thought they were a love match. So many attending this soiree at the governor's mansion thought far too highly of themselves. But she did not blame them for flirting with her. Emily coldly evaluated the other women present. Without a trace of braggadocio she knew she was easily the loveliest in the vast ballroom. Her fiery red hair was arranged in the latest style popular back in Boston, her hometown. Emerald eyes were sharp and clear and seemed to see all the way to the Emerald Isle itself.

Her dress made the territorial women's look dated, even primitive and more worthy of something to do the laundry in. A scoop neck plunged daringly, revealing the surge of her snowy white breasts. Not too much, not enough to be scandalous, but certainly more than the frontier ladies revealed. With good reason. She displayed what they didn't have, or not worth mentioning, at any rate.

She spoke like Main Line society back East, wore fashions

only beginning to appear in Colorado—with luck, at least the new governor's wife might have something approaching Emily's haute couture when the territory became a state. Somehow, Emily doubted it. The inaugural ball would be a dreary thing compared to functions in Washington and New York. And, of course, Boston.

"Miss O'Connor, may I have this dance?" The gentleman held out his hand. Emily graced him with a smile.

"Of course, Governor Routt, you may. It will be my great pleasure to let you ... lead."

This brought the appropriate smile to the man's lips. She tucked away her fan and gracefully twirled about so that his extended arm circled her waist. From the corner of her eyes she saw the wave of feminine disapproval. If the governor's wife hadn't been giving her a stare designed to kill at twenty paces, she would have given him a light kiss on the cheek. There was no need to foolishly earn the older woman's animosity. Instead, Emily spun back and, arm extended, let him escort her to the dance floor.

The orchestra performed adequately for her taste. A waltz. Her favorite. She kept a chaste distance from the governor as they spun about the dance floor.

"Your home is the perfect spot for entertaining," she said. "Such lovely decor. Your wife's choice, am I correct? Please let her know her taste is exquisite." Before the governor responded, Emily added in a whisper, "But of course it must be. She chose you as her husband."

They bantered back and forth until the waltz ended. Emily tapped her fan against her left palm in a show of appreciation, opened it and said, "I must get to work."

"Work? Oh, the charity games," Governor Routt said. "I must have a few more dances with wives of men who will form my cabinet after statehood."

"You men are all alike. Nothing but work, work, work."

Emily laughed lightly and let the man fulfill the roster on his dance card. While the women had written dance cards, she knew the governor had an undisclosed mental one. Keep the wives happy and their husbands were more amenable to political jostling.

Emily thought the governor had danced with her because he wanted to, not through any sense of duty. After all, she held no reins of power. She smiled just a little. She held no leash to a husband who had such influence. All that was required of her was to run the charity collection for an orphanage sponsored by the Ladies Relief Society. This work on her part would soothe Mrs Routt's ruffled feathers. The Denver Orphans Home was to take care of the orphans brought to Colorado to build the railroads and work in the mines.

Considering the treatment of children that Emily had seen, she would work especially hard this evening to separate the upper crust of the Denver elite from as much money as possible. With her looks and her skill, not a one of the men would leave this soiree with two nickels to rub together.

She made her way through the ballroom, taking a champagne flute from a waiter along the way. She sipped at it. Only steely self control kept her from spitting it out. Grand Monopole it was not. For all she knew it was squeezed from mine tailings and put into a champagne bottle for such social events. The frontiersmen had much to learn of putting on a decent ball.

She poured the champagne into a potted plant, gave a silent prayer that the plant survived, then returned the empty flute to a tray. She delicately dried her lips to remove the last trace of the foul tasting liquid. A quick look around convinced her that asking for a shot of bourbon was out of the question. During her high society upbringing hard liquor had never touched her lips, but *he* had shown her how the finest Kentucky product was fine, indeed.

Him.

Emily patted her hair to be certain it was in place, made sure the few pearls scattered about the ocean of red surging hair were properly displayed, then rounded the faro table and studied the layout. She expected the cards to be pristine and the table itself to be brand spanking new. Instead, someone had borrowed--or confiscated--the table and cards from some gambling den. Emily fanned the cards out on the table, squared them and ran her sensitive fingers along the edges.

A smile came to her lips. She wondered if whoever had furnished the layout knew the cards were shaved. Given a few minutes of practice she could deal any hand she desired. Putting the cards aside, she opened another sealed deck. A quick riffle showed how these cards were marked.

"Getting the feel of the pasteboards?"

She looked up and smiled automatically. The well-dressed man graced her with an open gaze of appreciation for her beauty. Emily wished she was on the other side of the table to bump into him, let her hands do some surreptitious searching, or otherwise to find if he carried a gun. As far as she could tell, he was unarmed, but he had the look of a feral creature. He ought to carry a pistol or at least a knife.

"I'll start the game in a few minutes, after the governor finishes his speechifying."

"Speechifying? I like that. It suits Governor Routt well." The man reached out, straining a bit more than was called for my etiquette to take her hand and shake it. If the faro table hadn't separated them, Emily was certain he would have kissed her hand. "I am Paul Vandenberg."

He said it as if she knew instantly who he was. She decided he was another of the minor politicians with an inflated sense of his own importance. The room was crowded with them. This close to Colorado becoming a state, they all intended to move up in the power structure. The only one she was sure of attaining his goal was territorial Governor Routt. After the election, he would be John Long Routt, first governor of the state of Colorado.

"Charmed to make your acquaintance," she said. "Would you be so kind as to help me, Mister Vandenberg?" Chandeliers were hardly required in the ballroom anymore because of the way his face lit up.

"Anything, Miss O'Connor. Or may I call you Emily?"

She had been right about him. A politician. She hadn't given her name, yet he had inquired before coming over. She learned more and more about him every time he opened his mouth. She wondered what it would take to get him into a poker game. She'd have him cleaned out before sunrise.

"Let me run a practice game, just to be sure I understand the rules." She batted her eyelashes at him. Her green eyes noted the contracting small muscles around his mouth and eyes as he tried not to show his surprise.

"I am sure you will do well. Is this your first time to deal faro?"

"The rules seem simple enough." She shuffled the marked cards, placed a few face cards at the top of the deck for practice and dropped them in the shoe. "Let me see if they slide easily. Oh, yes, they do. It is a new deck, after all. There's no reason for them not to just fly out."

She burned the first card, and said, "I believe this is referred to as the soda card. Am I right?" She saw his confusion. He nodded. "Oh, good. I learned that much. Go on. Place a bet, just for practice."

As he dropped a twenty-dollar gold piece onto his bet, Emily drew two cards.

"This is my card. Well, the banker's card." She dropped it to the right of the card box. "And now for yours as player.

You get this one." She put a second card to the left of the shoe.

"Oh, sorry, Mister Vandenberg, the banker's card matches yours. You lose." She reached out to take his double eagle.

He placed his hand atop hers.

"Are you sure you haven't played this before?"

"Why, sir—Paul. This is the first time I've ever run a bank in the governor's mansion."

"Do you permit coppering?"

She answered before thinking. "Contribute a penny and I'll use that. But that only allows you to change whether your card is above or below—matching the banker's card is a loss."

"I feel I am being hustled," he said. She saw he was displeased at the notion.

"Oh, Paul darling, this is for charity. All the money won by the bank goes to the orphans." She turned her hand over and pressed his to the felt table. "I am sure the players will gladly contribute winnings, too, so everything crossing this table is a winner—for the orphans."

Before he had a chance to reply, a woman came up and took his arm, snuggling against him. If Emily hadn't been present this would have been the belle of the ball. The daggers she shot in the redhead's direction made it clear that she wasn't going to relinquish anything else. Paul Vandenberg was her property.

"Paul, dear, do come and meet some of the railroad men." She pointedly turned so her shoulder shut Emily out of the conversation.

Emily disengaged her hand and said, "Why not play a hand or two? It's so simple. You bet and try to get over the dealer's card."

"Or under if you copper the bet," Paul Vandenberg said.

"That sounds so ... complicated," the woman said.

"I'm sure your husband will be happy to coach you,"

Emily said. She blinked in surprise. The reaction was not as she expected. These two weren't married. The ostentatious diamond ring on the woman's finger showed she was. That hinted at an illicit affair. Emily wasn't one to blackmail, especially over such sexual peccadilloes, but it gave her more insight into how the Denver Capitol functioned. Knowledge was power. If necessary, she was sure she could get any favor she wanted from Vandenberg.

"My husband *never* gambles. Not on cards. He owns the Cheyenne-Denver Railroad, you know. Horace Toms. I am sure you've heard of him." She looked down her nose at Emily.

"How wonderful for you, being able to travel from Cheyenne to Denver and back and not have to pay for a ticket," Emily said sweetly.

Vandenberg held back a chuckle, then put on what he thought was a poker face. Emily so wanted to play high stakes poker with him all the more.

"Come along, Clarissa. I wanted to introduce you to the governor's wife." Paul Vandenberg steered her from the table.

As they left Emily heard the railroad magnate's wife boast, "You know so many important people, Paul. Why shouldn't you? You're destined for such important things with Governor Routt once Colorado is granted statehood. I'll be sure that Horace rewards you for your fine ... service."

Emily almost burst out laughing and called, "Your fine servicing," but she held back the retort. She did have a civic duty to perform this evening, and infuriating a rich railroad magnate's wife and her boyfriend got in the way.

Emily returned the cards to the deck and shuffled them. After she loaded the shoe, she had learned the markings well enough to predict the outcome of any bet. In a way, she felt dejected. She had been hired to deal. The fifty dollars promised her by the governor wasn't going to increase if she bilked everyone out of their bets or if the bank failed to show a profit. She had been right telling Paul Vandenberg that losers would be cheerful at how they had contributed and winners would push back their money to feel good about their generosity.

It hardly surprised her that the well-dressed men professed ignorance of the game, yet bet cunningly. The women with them similarly enjoyed the thrill of winning, especially from Emily O'Connor. For them the reward was less the payoff and more that they had shown her up, with her Bostonian ways and dress that put theirs to shame. Emily was only too happy to oblige them. After all, her pay was divorced from the betting and the banker's success.

She flirted and made small talk and egged on bigger stakes from those movers and shakers of Denver commerce. After two hours, she estimated the bank had netted more than a thousand dollars. Before the end of the ball, the winners would be lined up to add to the amount. She felt she had done her civic duty, even if she was the only one leaving the table with more money than they had begun.

Emily began putting away the equipment when a shadow fell on the table.

"Sorry, sir, we're closed down. If you'd like to donate ... " Her voice trailed off as she looked up and saw the immaculately dressed man towering on the other side of the table. The guests wore white tie and evening garb. This one dressed down from that, yet showed more style and class than any of the other guests.

"If you are closed, let's leave. I have a carriage waiting. It'd be a shame to sully such a lovely gown with evening dew if you walked." She said nothing so he went on, "Such finery must have cost several hundred dollars. And the pearls in your hair? I haven't seen them before. Their shine tells me they are real."

"They're real. I chose white rather than black because they have a special sheen."

"And black wouldn't highlight your gorgeous red hair." He held out his arm.

"I should pay my respects to the governor and--"

"I've done that for you. John and I need to talk at length, but not now. Now, *we* need to discuss your future."

"Very well," she said. She looped her arm through Allister Legende's, and they left the governor's soiree. Emily saw the women were pleased at her departure. She wished she had a copper to turn the result. She wanted to be pleased at staying, even in such a field of weeds, since leaving meant nothing good was going to happen to her.

※ 5 ❀

F rank Landry paced about the library, pretending to read the book titles. The few he actually noticed were in languages he didn't speak. The ones in English hardly appealed to him that much more. Even when he came to a small section devoted to distilling, he walked past. He disliked being held a prisoner, and that was exactly his present condition.

It hardly mattered that a butler attended his every want. A small cut crystal decanter on a marble-topped table by the window contained a decent whiskey. More than decent, he discovered by sipping at a glass. As much as he'd have liked to knock back the shot and work his way to the bottom of the decanter, he restrained himself. Keeping sober and alert counted for more now.

Besides, he was a whiskey peddler and had bottles equaling the quality being offered. He rounded the table and looked out the bay window into the well-kept yard. A gardener tended some bushes, but something about the man seemed wrong. It took Frank a second look to decide that even the gardener working away in the twilight was well heeled. From the bulge at the small of his back, hidden by a long work coat, he carried something at least as large as a Peacemaker.

"What can I call you?" Frank turned from the yard man to Mister Small, standing with his huge arms crossed over a chest more like a whiskey barrel than anything a human being ought to possess. No matter where he went as he circled the room, Mister Small's deep-set eyes followed him. Frank had seen coiled springs that were less tense and ready to explode.

"You know my name. It hasn't changed since we arrived."

"Yes, the Society of Buckhorn and Bison, whatever that is," Frank said. "I meant that there's no reason we can't be on more casual terms. Call me Frank." He went to Mister Small and thrust out his hand. The towering man made no move to accept the proposed gesture of friendship. "You have a first name. Let's use our first names. Relax. Join me in a drink. The whiskey is very good, and I should know."

"No."

Frank frowned.

"No what? No to telling me what your first name is or no to sampling some of our unknown host's bourbon?" He touched his holster, considering his chances of drawing, shooting down the man so intent on guarding him and escaping this house. Even if he brought Mister Small down, the butler was outside. The gunshot would bring him running, his weapon cocked and ready. And the gardener. He was more than a common workman.

"No."

The denial settled the matter of hospitality and cordiality. Frank continued to circle the room. He stopped in front of a bookcase that seemed different. After a full minute examining it, he ran his fingers along the underside of a shelf. He pressed a release. Half the wall rolled outward to reveal a small room with four chairs around an oval table.

He stuck his head in and looked around. Exquisite oil paintings by European masters decorated the walls. Tables at the far corners held ornate kerosene lamps, but he doubted they were used. A crystal chandelier swung gently from the breeze he introduced by opening the hidden door.

"Should we go in for our conference?"

Mister Small shrugged and said nothing. Frank poked around in the room but found nothing unusual, except that it was a secret room off the library. He exited and pushed the shelving back into place with a small click.

"You don't care if I explore?" His guard said nothing, but he had allowed his prisoner to open the secret panel. Frank continued to search the room. A second section of bookcase looked as if it concealed a secret room, too, but Frank worked several minutes without finding the release. He finally gave up, not because he was wrong about there being another exit from the room but because he was tiring of being penned up.

"I'm going to leave now," he said. He drew back his coat and cleared his six-shooter. Even if it took all six rounds to stop Mister Small, he was willing now to do it.

"Mister Legende is back," the giant said unexpectedly. He opened the door from the library and gestured for Frank to precede him into the foyer.

Frank wished he had a better appreciation of artwork and statuary. The hidden room off the library was exquisitely decorated, but the foyer held artwork better suited for fancy museums back East. For a moment he was turned around and started deeper into the house, past the broad staircase winding up to the second floor. The butler announced him, causing Frank to spin around and face the tall, somber man. But he hardly noticed Allister Legende.

"Emily!"

"Frank!"

They stared at each other in disbelief. Both said at the same instant, "What are you doing here?"

Frank broke away from that lame exchange and began a steady cursing, detailing the redhead's least desirable traits. She drowned him out with her own denunciation.

"Please, silence!" Legende had to repeat his sharp order. "I hadn't realized you knew each other."

"He--"

"She--"

"Quiet, please." This time Legende's words carried the snap of a military command. He turned to the butler and spoke rapidly. The butler blanched, half bowed and backed off. Legende sucked in a deep breath and once more addressed his guests. "There has been a grievous error. I apologize."

"He made it?" Frank saw how pale the butler remained. "What was he supposed to do? Find out about her?"

"Your histories failed to mention knowing one another." Legende silenced them with a raised hand. "From your, shall we say, greeting statements, we certainly did not realize you had been married."

"It's nothing I want known." Emily drew herself up and glared at her ex-husband.

Frank pressed his hand over the glass-enclosed four-leaf clover to keep her from seeing it.

"And I certainly don't brag on making such a terrible mistake. Now, sir, I will take my leave." Frank moved but Mister Small blocked his way.

"Then I'll leave," Emily said. Kingston closed the door and made a point of bolting it.

"Put your mutual animosity aside for the time being. You were chosen for a specific task, one that will pay quite well. Hear me out."

"We can leave if we don't like what we hear? I haven't

appreciated our previous meeting." Frank saw how Emily exchanged hushed words with Kingston. They knew each other. That meant she and Legende were also acquainted. That intrigued him since he had never suspected Emily of traveling in such exalted circles.

A look around made him estimate the value of the art, of the house, of everything he had seen. Legende was well off. Very well off. He had come a long way since their trails had crossed before.

"I'll give you a minute to convince me," Frank said.

"I want to go, Allister. There's nothing here for me."

"You'll stay, Emily. You owe me."

"She borrowed money from you? That's rich. Why'd you give such a reprobate like her so much as a buffalo nickel? You're lucky she didn't skip town and stick you for the entire amount." Frank saw Emily's reaction and knew he had come close to the truth. "How much did she borrow?"

"The money was lost in a poker game," Legende said. "Please, come this way so I can tell you why your cooperation is vital."

"Vital? That kind of word means life or death," Emily said. "You've made a big mistake including *him*. He lacks the courage to ever engage in anything that important."

"You were the one who ran out on me," Frank snapped.

"After you cheated on me with that New Orleans trollop."

"She was a French contessa!"

"We were married!"

Frank started toward Emily, only to find the way blocked by Mister Small. He tried to dodge but for a man his size, Mister Small was surprisingly quick. When he took a step forward, he pushed Frank in front of him.

"The conference room. Now," Allister Legende said.

Frank let himself be herded back to an ornately carved door at the end of the hallway. Kingston used an oversized key to open the lock. The door swung inward on silent hinges. A huge conference table dominated the room, with comfortable chairs drawn up around it. A ten-foot wide fire-place behind the table was hardly noticeable. Dominating the space above it were buckhorn and bison heads. Frank tried to seat himself as far from Emily as possible, but Mister Small held out a chair to Legende's right while Kingston performed a similar ritual for Emily on the man's left side.

In front of Legende on the table a closed plain pine box about the size suitable for a pair of pistols obviously contained the reason they had been "invited" to the Society of Buckhorn and Bison council chamber.

"You have both had a chance to see the house. It is our Society headquarters."

"It's got plenty of secret rooms," Frank Landry said. Emily was not startled by this.

"And secret passages," she added.

"That is one feature of our headquarters," Legende said. "For members, we hide nothing. You will be free to explore as you see fit. There are rooms on the third floor suitable for residence, should you choose to live here."

"It's a hotel?" Frank was surprised at this.

"Not at all. Only members in good standing are permitted to stay here." Legende fixed Frank with a cold stare. "That includes overnight guests."

"What's she told you? It's--" Frank got no farther. Legende spoke over his protests.

"The Society accepts assignments from a highly placed official in Washington that require finesse, daring and, sometimes, sacrifice. Be assured these assignments are never haphazard or trivial. They all deal with threats to the country that only Society members are capable of meeting with any degree of success."

"Will you forgive my gambling debt if I do whatever it

takes to complete this, as you call it, assignment?" Emily looked determined.

Frank wondered how she had lost such a significant sum to Allister Legende. Her skill was phenomenal, the best he had ever seen. Legende must have enjoyed a run of luck to beat her unlike anything ever known in the world of cards.

Legende stared at him as if reading his mind. The man said, "I won on a bluff."

Frank sank back into the padded chair. He expected Emily to argue. When she didn't, he realized there were layers of skill above even what his former wife possessed. That hit him like a blow to the gut.

"I don't owe you any money. What can you pay me? I'm only a whiskey peddler and not a gun slick."

"Your skills are exactly those needed. I received this case file." Legende opened the pine box and drew out a stack of newspaper clippings and a sheet filled with several columns written in a small, precise hand. Legende passed the clippings out, Emily taking a few and Frank the rest. He kept the hand-written instructions.

"Colorado will become a state as soon as the vote goes through Congress. Approval by the territorial legislature is done and a popular vote is only a formality. The political figures involved are obvious. John Routt will become Governor Routt and a new legislature will mirror the existing one for the territory."

"Who's this Carlton Clark?" Emily pushed the clippings toward Frank. He hadn't finished scanning the ones he held. "I've never heard of him."

"He is something of a fly in the ointment," Legende said. "He opposes Colorado statehood and is willing to fight to keep it independent." He flipped through the papers in the box and flipped a card onto the table. "He and his army of desperadoes robbed a train of a considerable amount of gold. They slaughtered everyone aboard, and he left this."

"What's the Nation of Auraria?" Frank let Emily see it. She paid scant attention to it.

"He obviously sees himself as governor of a new state," she said. "Auraria, not Colorado."

"More like he envisions himself as king of a new country. His ambitions are as large as his conceit. However, he is a dangerous man. With the huge amount of gold stolen in the robbery, he can recruit an army capable of matching anything the US government can field, at least for the foreseeable future. Eventually the US Army will prevail, but the death and destruction reaching that point will be unacceptable."

"He's a colonel," Frank said, finally reading a clipping. "What's his military record?"

"That is something of a mystery. He engaged in two fili-busters that we know of, one to Nicaragua with that fool William Walker and another after the Civil War to Costa Rica. At least we think so. There is ample evidence that Clark is not his real name."

"Where did he get promoted to colonel? With the CSA?"

"He might have fought as a rebel, but he might have been cashiered for cowardice from a Union battalion, too. His history is murky."

"So he is falsely claiming the rank?" Emily looked thoughtful. "That gives some insight into the man's infe-riority."

"He might believe the history he tells his ruffians. I cannot call them soldiers. They are as far from troopers as possible." Legende took a scrap of paper from the box and handed it to Emily. "This was found in the freight car. Clark apparently used the combination to open the safe without recourse to blowing it apart."

"Who gave it to him?" Emily smiled wryly. "That's what

you want me to find out. Other than the depot agents, who knew the combination?"

"We don't know but suspect the railroad officials did, not because of this gold shipment but for prior documents being shipped. You've already met him, haven't you? Horace Toms?"

"I didn't meet him, but I did have a run-in with his wife, Clarissa."

"That figures," Frank said. "Always ready for a cat fight."

"Is it possible Mister Toms gave Clark the combination? He might desire more from life than having his own parlor car. A cushy bed in the governor's mansion might be in the cards, or so he thinks." She looked pleased with herself at unearthing the conspirator so quickly.

"That, Emily, had not occurred to me. You will find out." Legende turned to Frank. "And you will infiltrate Colonel Clark's little army. We know almost nothing about its size, the quality of training or what tactics they will use to seize power."

"Why me?"

"You've got a silver tongue, you fox, you," Emily said. "Why, you can sell the worst tarantula juice at premium prices and coax even an unwilling contessa into your bed." Emily smiled wickedly.

"Disregarding the latter part of that," Legende said, "she is correct. Your skill at spinning tales allows you to sell a product to saloon owners disinclined to buy a drop of your product. Sell yourself to Clark. Perhaps you can convince him that you have armaments for sale. No matter how well armed his militia is, they can always use more modern weapons, heavier cannon, anything he doesn't have."

"I can't sell something I don't have. Clark may be lying about his background, but he's not a stupid man if he stole a train filled with gold or recruited enough men to make such a theft possible."

"My connections will get you whatever you need to convince him."

"A howitzer? A Gatling gun?"

"Those, Spencers, ammunition, promise the moon. We will back you up." Legende began returning the clippings and papers to the box, as if he considered the matter settled.

"Why not have Mister Small infiltrate? He's probably more experienced." Frank looked up at the hulking man standing near the exit. "Never mind. You need someone who's less ... conspicuous."

"Mister Small makes an excellent resource, should you need support. You are correct in that he draws attention, thanks to his size." Legende began replacing the material in the box. He read down the handwritten sheet a final time, then added it to the contents. "The slip found next to the safe, please?"

"Let me keep it," Emily said. "It was torn from a larger sheet. I doubt I can match it with the full sheet, but the paper seems distinctive." She rubbed her fingers over it.

"Very well. You realize that Colonel Clark and whoever wrote the combination will recognize this as evidence against them. The slaughter of all the passengers and crew on the train show they have no remorse." Legende thought for a moment, then added, "They also wiped out another gang attempting to hold up the train. We found eight bodies riddled with bullets. None of them were crew or passengers."

"What else are you not telling us?" Frank asked.

"One of the robbers looked to have been shot through the head with a single round fired from a considerable distance. Whoever did it is a remarkable marksman."

"Great. I have to dodge a sniper to get close enough to sell guns that don't exist to a power mad crazy man pretending to be a soldier."

"That sounds like a job right up your alley, Frank." Emily grinned wickedly.

"She gets her debt wiped out. You never said what's in it for me." Frank saw how Legende reacted.

"Life is becoming dull for you. I offer excitement. And membership to the Society of Buckhorn and Bison."

"About that," Frank said. He stood and went to the fireplace. "What's the story about these?"

Six cartridges of different calibers were lined up under the buckhorn and bison heads.

"Each member of the Society leaves a round on the mantle while active. Please put one of your .36 rounds in the line." Legende turned to Emily and asked for one of her .45 derringer rounds. With exaggerated precision, he placed it at the end of the line next to a .22 cartridge.

Frank made a point of adding his .36 round at the other end.

"I can guess who this one belongs to." He tapped the mantle in front of a huge .50-90 Sharps round. Frank Landry looked over his shoulder at Mister Small. He stiffened when the giant shook his head slowly and held out a Colt New Line .22 caliber pistol.

"Then who ...?"

Frank stared at Allister Legende, the big gun in the Society of Buckhorn and Bison.

❧ 6 ❧

W hy're you back?" Joseph sidled away to get as far from Frank Landry as possible. It hardly mattered that the long oak bar separated them.

Frank Landry tipped his hat and smiled winningly. A quick look around the Oak Bucket Saloon convinced him this was the spot to find out what he needed to know. A half dozen customers were scattered around. Two had passed out. The other four were being ignored by the soiled doves. They were either too poxy to consider, which was something that made him a bit leery to even be in the same room, or more likely, they were down to their last dime.

"I wanted a fine drinking emporium. Where better in Denver than the Oak Bucket?"

"You cleaned me out. I don't have any money left. There's nothing more of yours I can buy." Joseph inched farther away and stopped about where Frank thought the barkeep stashed a sawed-off shotgun behind the bar.

"Then let me sample some of the fine liquor I sold you and return a few coins to your till."

"A shot?"

"A half bottle," Frank said. This perked up the nearest Cyprian. She smiled. He wished she hadn't. A blackened front tooth and its missing mate ruined her beauty. "Bring it to whatever table she's at." He pointed to where the woman stood, waiting for a customer.

"I'll be glad to service you," she said. The washed out blonde hurried to the bar and grabbed the bottle Joseph set on the bar. She took two shot glasses and returned.

"You're Frank. I remember you from yesterday."

He let her pour a couple fingers into the glass. The amber booze was a mite lighter in color than when he had sold it to Joseph the prior day. It hadn't taken long to water it down to get even more than 26 shots from a bottle. He raised the glass in salute to his winsome drinking partner and downed it in a single gulp. The smoothness remained, but the kick wasn't as potent. Joseph had definitely watered the liquor. At least he hadn't added rusty nails to give it body. Frank thought he'd have to congratulate him for that wise decision.

"I'm Denise," the woman said. She tugged at her dress so more of her breasts showed, at least the bare tops.

"That de-nice," he said.

She smiled uncertainly and said, "That's a joke, ain't it? Denise, de-nice?"

"Of course it is. It takes a woman of great wit to understand." Frank hoped lightning wouldn't strike him for such blarney.

"I'll drink to that," she said, eagerly pouring another shot. He let her down it while nursing his. Trying to drink her under the table was a fool's errand. Better to expect a few drinks loosened her tongue.

The idle talk meandered all around. When Denise had consumed most of the liquor, Frank steered the conversation in the direction he desired.

"You know I'm a whiskey peddler. I also sell other things."

She smiled drunkenly.

"So do I, Frank. You wanna see what I got to sell?" She started to lift her skirts. Frank suspected she didn't wear anything underneath. He caught her wrist and forced her to keep her skirts down, if not at a demur height then not at a scandalous one.

"I've come into a shipment that's not what you'd call legal."

"Moonshine? I grew up in Kaintuck. My uncle made the best 'shine in the hollow, even if some of the folks went blind." She smiled her toothless smile. "Thas how we knowed it was good."

"What I came across gives a bigger bang—a different bang." He held up his thumb, used his index finger as a barrel and silently went "pow!"

"Oh, you mean guns?"

"Rifles. Maybe something bigger."

"Bigger? Cannon? I heard tell of how they sound when they go off. Mount Sterling was a big battle in the war. My cousins from that part of the state tole me 'bout how loud cannons sound when they go off. Roar!" She threw up her arms and almost fell from the chair. Frank caught her and pulled her back.

"That's what I'm talking about. If I sell them for enough, there'd be a commission in it for whoever put me in touch with a buyer." He saw the concept was too complicated for Denise. "You could make a pile of money helping me find a buyer."

"Me and you? Partners? Thas good."

"It certainly can be. Might be," he said. "Have you heard anybody in the saloon talking about cannons and rifles and things?"

She hiccuped. Her bloodshot eyes went out of focus for a moment, then fixed on his sharp blue ones.

"You wouldn't cheat me, would you, Frank?"

"Never, my dear, never." He kissed the back of her hand, this being the cleanest part he could see. "Is it somebody in here now?" He cast a look at the men who were passed out. Neither would be much good. The others didn't have the swagger he expected of someone offering hundreds or even thousands of dollars for stolen arms.

"He comes in now and again. Big talker, treats us girls poorly, but he's got money. Flashes it around. He had a pocket of greenbacks last time he got drunk."

"Who is this?" Frank poured the last of the whiskey into Denise's glass. She looked at it with real sorrow in her eyes. The bottle was empty. A quick move drained the shot glass. She looked at him expectantly. "I'll get another if you can tell me where to find Mister .... " He let his sentence trail off.

She completed it for him.

"Blackmun. Thas what he calls hisself. If he ain't here, he's across the street at the Whore."

"The whore?"

"The Whore of Babylon. A real dive. Wouldn't be caught dead in there. Too many *are* made dead there. Rough crowd." Denise belched and wiped her mouth with her hairy forearm.

It took another few minutes to wheedle Blackmun's description from her, though much of it did Frank no good. What Blackmun looked like without his pants on mattered less than how to spot him as he leaned against a bar. He decided attitude was a better guide to find the man than the size of his Denise-pleaser.

He swung his case through the door into the Babylon and sized up the barkeep. The man looked like a rat. Frank smiled. Offer a rat a piece of cheese and you had him. He went to the bar and started to order.

"All we got's beer. You want anything else, go somewhere else."

"Then I'll have a beer." Frank started to give his pitch. He was a whiskey peddler, after all, and enjoyed the pursuit of a sale where none had been made before. But something deterred him. He dropped a nickle on the bar and looked askance at the glass of beer. The foam head was thin and the color made him leery, but when he sipped it he was pleasantly surprised. It wet his whistle. Luck in this meant luck elsewhere. He started to call to the barkeep and ask after Blackmun when he chanced to overhear two men at a table behind him. Trying not to obviously eavesdrop, he half turned and rested his elbow on the bar as if sizing up the ladies working the back of the room.

None of them matched the quality Denise had shown across the street in the Oak Bucket. As he worked on his beer, he cast a sidelong look at the two men. They hunched over the table, sitting side by side so neither had to have his back to the door. Rather than suspicious, Frank considered this prudent in an establishment with this ambience. They weren't looking directly at him, but he wasn't able to see their faces, either. While they spoke in a low tone, he was able to hear enough to interest him.

Frank had considered asking about selling arms he didn't have to flush out Blackmun or someone else who might be connected with Colonel Clark's militia. He overheard the opposite deal. The one tried to sell arms for the other to buy. Adding a middleman to such an illicit deal kept Frank safer.

"You got that many rifles? Where'd you come by them?"

"Don't ask. I got them. And more. We got mountain howitzers, too. And the 12-pound balls for them. You can blow open a bank vault with a single shot."

"They're that powerful?"

"They beat the Apaches back for years. General Crook swears by 'em."

"How much?" The buyer turned a little, giving Frank a better look. He didn't have a good description for Blackmun, but if he had, this would be what he'd expect. The coal-black eyes burned with a ferocity bordering on madness. A big dark mustache dotted with his last meal wiggled about as if his lip had developed the palsy.

More telling, the man wore two six-shooters, each slung in a cross-draw holster. Denver was a wild and wooly town, but there wasn't a great need to carry two six-guns. From the look of the irons, they were used hard and often.

"Five hunnerd for a howitzer."

"How much for a half dozen?"

If Frank had any question about the mustachioed man, this erased it. Buying one cannon was unusual, but no one needed that many unless they intended to go to war.

"Six? You want six?" The seller sounded amazed. Frank also caught something else in the man's tone that the buyer whom he took to be the Blackmun fellow Denise had identified missed. "Not a problem. I can give you a discount for that many. Five hundred for each but I'll throw in some grapeshot and gunpowder."

"I need rifles, too. How many can you get me?"

"As many as you want. I've got a great pipeline that goes all the way back to the Federal armories back East."

"Five hundred rifles."

Again Frank heard an element of glee rather than skepticism in the man offering the weapons. They lowered their voices and Frank missed the asking price, but Blackmun didn't bother dickering.

"I got a down payment here." Blackmun pulled out a wad of greenbacks large enough to choke a cow. The other man dropped his hat over the scrip.

"You got the entire amount for the guns? Or just this?"

"I got more outside."

The two stood and left, Blackmun stuffing his money back into his coat pockets. Frank tossed down the rest of his beer, wishing he had time for another. It was rare finding such good brew anywhere, much less in a dive like this. The barkeep started for him to make the offer. Frank touched the brim of his hat and called, "Later, my friend. I congratulate your brewer on his fine product."

He hefted his case and pushed through the doors into the street. Finding Blackmun or someone who provided as good a lead as Blackmun might had been sheer luck. Frank had made the mistake of believing Lady Luck continued to look over his shoulder. Neither of the men from the saloon was in sight.

Panic was quickly replaced by anger. He started to his right, then stopped and looked at the buildings. They were tightly pressed together. The men had disappeared too quickly unless they had ducked into another of the saloons or bawdy houses. But that hadn't been their intent. A quick about face took him in the other direction where occasional alleyways between the stores and saloons gave more hope for finding the men in their illicit dealings.

The first space between buildings was too narrow for a man to walk down. Frank hurried on, then stopped. If luck had abandoned him, cold logic had given him back his lead. At the far end of the alley, the one he took to be Blackmun and the other man stood nose to nose, as if about to whale away at each other.

Frank left his whiskey case behind a rain barrel and cautiously made his way down the litter-strewn alley. If either of the men had turned, they would have seen him. Their argument was too engrossing.

"... said you had the guns!" Blackmun grabbed the man by his coat lapels and shook him hard.

69

"Whoa, rein back, mister. I said I knew how to put you in touch with the supplier. Pay me my commission, and I'll give you directions."

Blackmun shook harder and shoved the man back. Frank pressed against the nearest wall when Blackmun drew. He had seen gunslicks in his day. Some were fast but couldn't hit the broad side of a barn if they were locked in it. Others were slower but far more accurate. Blackmun had both guns out and fired. At such close range he couldn't miss. But it looked as if he did.

Or it seemed that he had missed until Frank saw what the gunman had done. Both muzzles were pressed to the gun seller's ears. Firing that close would deafen him. Frank noticed something else. The hot gun barrels branded both of the man's ears. He clamped his hands over them and whimpered like a whipped dog.

"You got the guns or not?" Blackmun had to shout.

The wounded man bobbed his head up and down.

"Let's take a look at them. Come on." Blackmun jerked the man around and shoved him back down the alley. He was intent on his prisoner, and the gun seller was in no condition to notice Frank beating a hasty retreat.

Frank popped out in the street, grabbed his whiskey case and looked around. His horse was back at the Society headquarters. He had come into the rougher part of Denver without it to keep the gelding from being stolen. His tack alone would draw the attention of every thief and cutthroat in a mile radius.

He put his head down and started to run. Without a horse there wasn't any way to follow the men.

"Mister Landry."

Hearing his name caused him to whirl about. Mister Small stood in shadow, the reins to Frank's horse in his monstrous hand. He held them out.

"I'll look after the liquor case."

"Come with me. I've found a man who--"

The giant shook his head and said, "I have something else to do for Mister Legende."

As much as Frank wanted the huge man riding with him, even if he carried a puny .22 pistol, he wasn't in a position to argue. He set down the case, tugged on Barleycorn's reins and forced the gelding to take a few steps. Frank vaulted into the saddle and rode into the street, looking around to see Blackmun forcing the gunrunner to mount his horse a hundred yards away.

He slowed Barleycorn to a walk as he headed in that direction. As intent as he was on Blackmun and his prisoner, Frank felt uncomfortable riding here. Hidden eyes followed his every move. Those eyes judged how much coin he had in his pocket, whether it was worth the effort to bushwhack him and steal everything or simply kill him for his horse and tack. With a tug, he pulled back his coat at his left hip, giving a clear path to drawing from his own cross-draw holster. Having the Colt handy now boosted his confidence. He still felt the appraising eyes, but they faded into insignificance.

Frank forced himself to come to a complete halt several times since Blackmun rode so slowly. They reached a cross street and turned north. As the buildings thinned out, the two men ahead of him rode faster. Frank gave Barleycorn his head and trotted along with growing confidence that he would discover the camp where Colonel Clark mustered his army. A quick report to Allister Legende so he could pass it along to whomever he answered to, and the assignment would be completed.

Frank would be accepted as a full-fledged member of the Society of Buckhorn and Bison, though that mattered almost nothing to him compared to finding the colonel before Emily. She was as obstinate and annoying as ever. Showing her up would put her in her place and give him bragging rights for years to come. Not that he intended to have any more to do with her after this matter was settled.

He fingered the glass-encased four-leap clover watch fob and smiled. It had stopped giving her luck and now bestowed grand fortune on him at last.

He tapped his heels on Barleycorn's flanks and brought the horse to a canter. The road turned to the northwest. Frank held back enough to avoid being obviously following, but enough others drove wagons and rode on horseback to provide cover for him. The road angled more sharply toward the Front Range and then went almost due north along the base of the towering mountains.

Just as he wondered if he was going to ride all the way to Wyoming, he lost the riders. He drew rein and studied the terrain ahead. The road dipped down and then rose again a few hundred yards farther north. Blackmun and his gunrunner must still be in the dip. Frank topped the lip of the depression and frowned. They weren't in sight.

He rode down the slope and almost missed the two sets of hoofprints riding across country, going toward higher country in the mountains. Frank made sure his gun rode easy and followed into undergrowth. A few trees dotted the area, giving him further cover. But if it hid him from their eyes, it also kept him from finding the two men.

He lost the tracks and began hunting on the debris-littered forest floor. The sound of horses--several horses--alerted him. He dropped to the ground and tethered Barley-corn to continue on foot. Winding through the stand of trees, he saw a small clearing where a half dozen horses were hobbled. From the McClellan saddles and the blankets branded with Army insignia, a squad of soldiers had dismounted.

"Go on, or retreat? What's the safest?" he softly asked

himself. Then he slid his pistol from its holster and continued his advance. Safety now mattered less than being able to lord it over Emily that he had brought Colonel Clark to justice. With luck, he might even find where the phony officer hid the bars of gold stolen from the train.

He stepped into another clearing, then quickly back-tracked. Blackmun had the gun dealer covered with his drawn six-gun. Frank moved through the edge of the forest, stepping carefully over dried bushes to keep from making too much noise, until he was with a dozen yards of the pair.

"Where is he? You got one minute for him to get here or I think you're a humbug and drill you!"

"Wait, don't shoot me," pleaded the gunrunner. "He'll be here. Honest."

"One minute. Make that thirty seconds." Blackmun lifted his six-gun and pressed the bore between the man's eyes.

"You're a suspicious cuss," boomed a voice that filled the glade. A sergeant marched from behind a tree only a few yards to Frank's right. He hadn't seen the non-com. Frank hunkered down and looked around. He was paying too much attention to the drama in the clearing and not enough about his surroundings.

"You're the one what can sell me the cannon and rifles?" Blackmun never moved his muzzle from the man's forehead.

"I can get you anything the army's got. If you have the money, I have the weapons."

"He's got a pocketful of bills, Sarge. I seen 'em."

"Shut up, Sterling. You haven't performed well so far. It's a good thing that Wylie saw you out on the road and alerted me. Would you have ridden straight to the fort with him if I hadn't given you the signal?"

"Sarge, please. I wouldn't have crossed you like that. He's got the money on him. I swear it."

"I've got scrip to feed the kitty," Blackmun said, "but payment will be in gold. All you can carry."

"I've heard that before," the sergeant scoffed. "Time to settle up."

"Settle up? I haven't dickered for the price yet. I told him that--" Blackmun jerked back when his prisoner's head exploded, spraying blood and brains all over him.

For an instant, Frank thought Blackmun's trigger finger had slipped. Then he saw a curl of smoke from a sniper's rifle in the forest. The sergeant had ordered the soldier to gun down their own man.

"Well, that cuts out the middle man," Blackmun said. "Now we can--"

A half dozen bullets ripped through him, staggering him. He got off a shot, but it went high and wild. Then he collapsed.

Frank swallowed hard. Six soldiers advanced from the woods, their rifles still smoking. The sergeant issued terse orders. He went through Blackmun's pockets and took out the sheaf of bills that had been flashed in the saloon. He stuffed the greenbacks into a pouch on his broad leather belt, then completed his search, taking anything of value.

"He was carrying a lot of money for someone who wasn't serious about buying guns. That means he might be missed. I don't want anybody hunting for him and finding him this near the fort." He searched the gunrunner more thoroughly and pocketed a few coins from a vest pocket, then unbuckled his gun belt and took his boots. The sergeant left, leading the dead soldier's man's horse and never casting a look back. It obviously didn't concern the murderous sergeant if this body was found. Maybe soldiers died this way all the time or maybe the sergeant had a way of explaining the man's absence from the fort. Whatever the explanation, Blackmun was the only one of concern.

Frank hunkered down as the other soldiers left, leading the horse carrying Blackmun, now tied over his saddle. He waited close to a half hour before making his way back to where he had tethered his gelding. Frank mounted and returned to the road, wondering what the hell he had gotten himself mixed up in for Legende.

Emily O'Connor lounged back in the comfortable chair, sipping the wine Kingston had poured. It didn't suit her taste, but she smiled and complimented his choice. That seemed to please him. Keeping the butler and especially Allister Legende happy mattered to her because of the money she owed. Legende claimed her poker loss would be wiped away if she saw this assignment through to its conclusion. Erasing a ten thousand dollar debt was not to be sniffed at, even if it did nothing to reduce the sting of finding that Legende had bluffed his way to winning that pot. How she had misread him was something that needed her careful attention.

It wasn't going to happen again.

"Assignment," she scoffed. The whole thing reeked of the sort of drama she disdained. Yet, looking around the library, this was more than petty tampering by someone bored with the way things were. Money had built the Society of Buckhorn and Bison, and Allister Legende showed a determination more of a competent employee than a man driven by personal ambitions or even boredom. This was not a sport, it was a job.

She finished the wine in a single gulp so its aftertaste wouldn't distract her. It was adequate, she decided, but not as good as Governor Routt served at his parties. She had attended enough in the past few weeks to know whose cellar she preferred.

"He wants to be elected Colorado's first governor," Legende said, appearing as if by magic. "I am sure he is using taxpayer money to buy only the finest."

Emily sat a little straighter in the chair. Frank had declared that the entire house was riddled with priests' holes, secret rooms and even hidden passages. She had dismissed his warning as an overactive imagination, perhaps what he would design into such a house. But Legende had somehow appeared in the library and she was watching the single door out into the foyer. It hadn't opened.

"I'm sorry the wine does not suit you," Legende said. He settled into the chair opposite hers.

"It's quite ... " She considered lying. That trail she took often during poker games looked unpromising in her current situation. Nothing slipped past Legende. "... quite awful, actually. It doesn't suit my palate."

"Unlike the whiskey Frank Landry sells?"

A flush rose to warm her cheeks, and she started to protest. Without any obvious summons, Kingston entered with a tray holding two pony glasses. She took the bourbon and settled back. A delicate sniff sampled the aroma. She wet her ruby lips with it and liked it. Dammit.

"Better, but still not great," she said.

Legende tasted his with more gusto. He licked his lips before setting the glass on the marble-topped table. Legende looked up. Kingston held out his tray again so his employer could slide off an envelope. The butler quietly left once this transfer was complete.

Legende glanced at the envelope as if to assure himself it was the right one, then handed it to Emily.

"This will get you into the governor's next party."

She looked at the engraved invitation with some appreciation.

"Gilt lettering. Very classy."

"The governor is serious about appealing to the territorial elites. With the backing of those who are impressed by such things"--he pointed to the invitation--"he will be a shoo-in as the state's first elected governor."

"If Colorado even becomes a state. What are Colonel Clark's chances for establishing the Nation of Auraria?"

"They must be good enough that our benefactor in Washington is worried."

"Worried enough to call out the big guns? The big guns in the Society of Buckhorn and Bison?"

Legende ignored her jibe.

"Attend this soiree tonight at the governor's mansion and find what you can about any opposition to statehood. While Governor Routt is strongly in favor of statehood, that doesn't mean everyone attending will be, also. If anything, such a gathering might bring out the opposition as they size up the governor's support. We must not assume that everyone on the governor's staff also endorses this change, either."

"Change means opportunity," she said. "Routt sees the change as Colorado becoming part of the United States. I am sure others would prefer to be King of Auraria, or whatever title they favor as ruler of an independent country. That is, if they are able to get rid of Colonel Clark. Or perhaps he will be the commanding general with someone else as figurehead? Or is he being used?"

"Your grasp of the situation is firm, and your conclusions match mine, Miss O'Connor. We need to find who the players are to find better solutions. Clark is not necessarily the major player in this sordid theater." Legende stood. Emily couldn't help but look up, way up, at him. His height commanded attention.

"Are you my escort? Or should I ask Kingston?" She enjoyed needling Legende to see his reaction. He had smoked her at their poker game because she had failed to read him. The more she prodded and dug and joked, the sooner a tell would reveal itself. Then she'd have him. But this wasn't that moment.

"I am otherwise occupied, as is Kingston. Would you like me to ask and see if Mister Small is available?" Legende laughed as he left her momentarily confused. Then she smiled ruefully. He had a sense of humor hidden away, unlike Frank Landry. The whiskey peddler showed no appreciation for light humor. At least not hers.

She sobered when she realized Legende played the same game she did, hunting for her weaknesses just as she probed for his.

She took the invitation, tucked it in a pocket in her skirts and left the society headquarters, thinking about her dress, how to present herself and not about an escort. She'd invite Mister Small before she asked Frank. After all, they were competitors. Stopping Colonel Clark before Frank even found where the man bivouacked his militia was her goal and, achieving it, she would have bragging rights for a long time.

As if she cared one whit about Frank Landry and his opinion.

SEA GREEN SUITED HER PERFECTLY. THE FLOWING SKIRTS swirled like waves breaking softly against the shoreline as she made her entrance. Every head in the ballroom turned. From the top of her fiery red hair to her ample bosom and narrow waist to the flaring pastel skirt, she was perfect. Emily smiled winningly, ignoring the women who hated her and directing her attention toward the men. Not having an escort made her all the more dangerous to the women—and appealing to the men.

She recognized many of the partygoers as current politicians and bureaucrats recruited by John Routt. Which of them might want to become grand ruler of a new nation in the middle of the US? Realistically, she knew the answer was all of them. Only Governor Routt himself was exempt from suspicion of being in league with Colonel Clark and his would-be filibusterers. From all she saw, Routt was popular enough to take over after the transition. Being the ruler of a petty nation was less desirable than governor of a full-fledged state opened to commerce and the right to appoint of two senators. Routt stood to increase local power onto a national stage. His counsel would be sought far quicker as governor than as self-proclaimed president of an independent country completely surrounded by US territory.

The mingling allowed her to drift from one group to another, listening, eavesdropping, gathering gossip. To her dismay, when she reached the far side of the room she hadn't learned anything worthwhile.

"Legende wasted his invitation," she said to herself in disgust. She snared a champagne flute from a passing waiter and looked out the window across Capitol Hill. This was the center of political power in Colorado, and she hadn't discovered a single thing. Nothing. She sipped the champagne and made a face. Her tastes were changing away from the bubbly wine. Frank's whiskey actually tasted better.

"It's not the finest vintage," came a familiar voice. She turned to Paul Vandenberg. "You are used to better back in Boston, I am sure."

"Mister Vandenberg," she said, lifting her half-filled glass in salute.

"Please. Paul."

"Of course, Paul. I am feeling at sixes and sevens tonight. It hardly seems possible, but I have been to so many of *these*," she said, making a sweeping gesture taking in the entire party, "that I am bored. Imagine being bored with a fine string quartet, such important people, even decent champagne." She drained her glass. Then she turned on her brilliant smile, looked Vandenberg in the eye and said in a lower voice, "Or such devastatingly handsome men as yourself, Mister Vandenberg."

"Paul," he said. "You can call me Paul."

"Only in the morning," she said in tone that promised the world.

"I look forward to hearing that whispered softly in my ear."

"There you are, Paul. I wondered where you'd gotten off to." Clarissa Toms seized his arm and half yanked him around. Emily wondered if the railroad magnate's wife would body slam the man and then go for a pin in the middle of the dance floor.

"Clarissa, you've met Miss O'Connor, haven't you?"

The woman looked down her nose at Emily and said, "Why, yes, I seem to remember seeing her before. Some-where tawdry, I am sure. Now come along, Paul darling. Horace is with a few men from the transcontinental lines I am sure you'd love to meet." She steered him away.

"Later, Paul," Emily called. "Perhaps in the morning?" She laughed when he jerked around to look at her, but Clarissa Toms had momentum on her side and kept him moving along.

She wished she could join that tight knot of men or at least be a fly on the wall near them. She recognized Horace

Toms as well as the vice-president of the Union Pacific and General Palmer, the owner of the Denver and Rio Grande railway. The three railroad executives would control commerce throughout Colorado far more than they already did once statehood was approved.

"Gold," she said softly, "flowing both east and west from Colorado. And crops." The vast farms in eastern Colorado would have markets opened back East. A few pennies per pound of transported freight poured immense wealth into these men's pockets.

None of the women paid her the least attention, at least not obviously. Many looked at her from the corner of their eye, judging her and scheming against her. The closest women moved closer to their escorts to keep this unwanted, redheaded predator from their territory. This was perfect for her next move.

Without needing to disengage from anyone, Emily had the opportunity to prowl about the governor's mansion. He had offices on the second floor and his living quarters on the third. What Routt knew or suspected about Colonel Clark would give important information to finding the rebel. If he knew nothing, Legende must inform him. If Routt had extensive information, some of it might not be known to Legende.

Emily made her way up the broad staircase, paused at the landing and looked back over the glitter and glamour below. Clarissa Toms glared at her. Emily blew her a kiss. The way the railroad magnate's wife jerked on Paul Vandenberg's arm made the evening a success.

Almost.

A real success would be gaining an idea of who, if anyone, opposed Governor Routt and sought to sell him out to Clark.

She found a hallway leading to the Routt's offices, but a liveried servant stood guard to keep errant guests from blindly wandering through the heart of the territory's governance. Emily considered how to approach the guard. Decoying him away would never do since he was sure to identify her. Being the belle of the ball had advantages. It was also a handicap if she wanted to rummage about in offices and not be seen or remembered.

Backing away, she started checking doors leading from the landing. All were locked. She tried to outguess the architect who had designed this luxurious mansion. At the far end away from the corridor leading to the offices, she discovered an unlocked door. She slipped into the room and tried to decide its purpose. A meeting room? Some convenient location for assignations of a forbidden nature?

She closed the door behind her and explored the room. It didn't offer any doors to adjoining rooms, but there were French doors onto a balcony. Emily had to jiggle the handle a few times to open the locked door, then stepped out into the cold Colorado night air. The Front Range loomed dark and ominous to the west while lights from Capitol Hill gave enough illumination for her to make her way along the balcony to a railing. A wide gap separated the end from another balcony. A quick estimate told her that was where she wanted.

The doors on the other balcony opened into the governor's office.

She drew up her skirts and clumsily sat on the railing, feet dangling down. Emily drew up her knees, found a secure spot on the outer side of the railing, then launched herself before her courage faded. A wild grab and she was dangling from the other balustrade. For any idle passerby in the grounds below she presented a beguiling picture. Struggling, she pulled herself up, flopped belly down over the railing, then kicked hard. She somersaulted over and landed with a thud on the flooring.

Emily sat up, brushed the dirt from her lovely skirts the

best she could, then stood to check the door into the governor's office. It was unlocked.

She slipped in and looked around the darkened room. The desk loomed like a child's fortress with tall stacks of paper forming the crenelation of a castle's battlements. Routt wasn't likely to leave whatever he had found about attempts to prevent Colorado from becoming a state in plain sight. Such information was more likely locked away.

Banks of file cabinets contained financial statements and other dreary forms, if the tags on the drawers were accurate. Those didn't interest her as much as the desk with its latched drawers. The center drawer yielded to her rattling and jiggling to slip the lock.

Emily scowled. As a spy she was getting nowhere. She closed the drawer and tried to rattle open a larger one on the right pedestal. This lock proved more secure. She found a letter opener and began prying. The drawer finally yielded to her crude lock picking attempts.

A file folder with a ribbon tied around it lay on top of the stack of other important looking leather-bound documents. She untied the ribbon and held it up to catch what light filtered in from outside.

"So, he knows about Clark," she said softly to herself. She scanned down the page. "And he suspects someone on his staff. Who? Who? It doesn't say."

"He won't find out, either."

Emily jumped at the voice, half turned and caught movement from the corner of her eye before a gag was drawn tight across her mouth. Trapped in the chair, she wasn't able to fight off her attacker. A blindfold was added to the gag and then a thumb and forefinger clamped down on her nose, cutting off her air.

She fought, but her efforts weakened until she blacked out.

❦   8   ❧

Colonel Clark trained his field glasses on the encampment below. It had taken more than a month of poring over scouting reports dating back to Zebulon Pike to find this bivouac for his troops. A narrow pass let men enter, though that passage was hardly as wide as a freight wagon. When he brought in the field pieces, he would use the other end of the canyon, that opened in a wide funnel to suck in a small river falling from higher altitudes. That river furnished his men with drinking water and basic sanitation.

He shook his head at that. They fought tooth and nail to keep from digging slit trenches and taking regular baths. Perhaps spending some of the gold he had been granted by the grace of the train robbery on uniforms would instill a better esprit de corps. When they went into battle, they would lack the long months of training required to match even the most slovenly US cavalry detachment. Orders to not shoot anyone wearing the olive green of the Nation of Auraria were easy to give, and even these nincompoops could remember. Blue? Shoot. Green? Your brother in arms.

But he didn't have the luxury of time for such training or to give his men proper uniforms. The rush to statehood required him to act swiftly if he wanted to prevent it.

Clark swept past the rows of cooking fires to get a better idea of the heights on the far side of the canyon. Any attack would come over the far rim and sweep down into his troops in a massive broadside attack. Small units posted at either end of the canyon bottled up any escape. He took out a note-book and made detailed notes, including a crude sketch of the camp and nearby mountains. This canyon opened at both ends but several branching canyons formed boxes. If his troops tried to retreat down any of them, they would be penned up and easily slaughtered. Better to develop tactics for driving the Federals into those box canyons where they could be annihilated.

Boots crunching into the gravel on the slope beneath him alerted him to someone approaching. The unwanted visitor made no attempt to walk quietly. He must be one of the AoA, the Army of Auraria. Just to be sure, Clark unbuttoned the flap of his holster and rested his hand on the six-gun's pearl handle. His instincts were true. He recognized the man slipping and sliding to climb the last few yards on the loose rock.

"There you are, Colonel. You should grow wings and fly if 'n you're gonna act like an eagle."

"Corporal Antrim, I gave orders not to be disturbed unless there was an emergency."

"Well, now, sir, me and the sergeant argued about that. I didn't hold to him sayin' it was that important, but he ordered me up here with the news."

Clark kept his temper. Antrim would get around to giving him the vital message in a minute. Or two. Sometime before the sun set.

"I see you got low-gist-ick-kul things to do. But it's about the captain."

"Blackmun bought the guns! Excellent. Is he in camp?"

"In a manner of speaking, Colonel. Well, not him exactly, but his horse is back."

"Where's Captain Blackmun?"

"Don't rightly know and can't say from just it bein' his horse trottin' in."

Corporal Antrim spoke to empty space. Clark worked his way down a path hidden from the canyon bottom. He was halfway back to camp before Antrim found the trail and followed, stumbling and cursing as he came.

Clark reached the edge of camp before he bellowed, "Sergeant! Report!"

One of the few men to have served in an actual army unit came over, his bowed legs almost comical. Anyone inclined to laugh at the cowboy's malady quickly thought differently seeing the cold pale eyes, the scarred face and the half-missing ear. Sergeant Giannini claimed it had been shot off in some military misadventure in northern Africa while serving with the French Foreign Legion, but it looked the world like somebody had bitten the ear off. Either explanation kept the others in his company from making fun of him or asking questions that might rile him.

"That's Captain Blackmun's horse. Where is the captain?" Clark squared off with his sergeant. Giannini didn't back down an inch.

"The damned horse came into camp without him. There's dried blood on the saddle and his saddlebags are gone. Looks like some fool tried to tie him into the saddle but the knots came loose."

Clark circled the captain's horse and reached the same conclusion. A few lengths of rope were secured to the saddle but stained where a man's legs might leak blood. The only conclusion he could reach was that he had lost Blackmun to some enemy. Since the captain had been in mufti and ordered to buy weapons, chances were good the killer knew nothing of the Army of Auraria and had only seen an easy theft.

He had warned that fool Blackmun about flashing wads of greenbacks. He might never have found an arms dealer, only a road agent or a swindler Denver was infamous for sheltering. When he became Premier of Auraria, he'd see to proper law enforcement, even if it meant every gas lamp in the city was used as a gallows for the thieves.

"Saddle up Bucephalus and assign three men to come with me."

"Should I join you, Colonel?" The sergeant looked fierce. "Me and the captain hit it off. I can't say we were friends, but me and him got along better 'n most."

"Who's left to command the troops?" Clark looked around as Antrim came huffing and puffing from the path down the mountain. "Corporal, go tell Lieutenant Zamora he is in charge until I return."

The corporal threw him a sloppy salute and shuffled away. Clark was undecided about Zamora. The man claimed to have been a colonel in the Federales and had grown tired of their corruption. Clark suspected the true reason Zamora had left Mexico had more to do with theft than politics. Whatever Zamora's reason for coming to Colorado, he was better trained than most of the soldiers. When Auraria became a free nation, Clark thought Zamora would make a decent governor of a small province, perhaps down south around Ouray where he could deal with the pesky Utes. Comments the Mexican expatriate had made around the campfire hinted that he was the man for the job.

"I figure the horse came from the main road through the pass," Giannini said, handing down the reins to Clark. "The horse remembered the way home."

"Or Blackmun tried to reach camp and fell from the saddle." He had to gentle Bucephalus. The stallion began crow hopping and trying to spin in circles to throw his rider. Clark knew the horse's tricks and let him wear himself out.

"That don't explain what happened to his saddlebags, Colonel. If he was trying to get back here, where'd they go?" Sergeant Giannini turned his mare's face toward the narrow notch leading out of the canyon.

Clark made sure his notebook was securely tucked inside his uniform coat and considered changing into less conspicuous clothing. After a few seconds weighing consequences, he put his heels to his horse's flanks and shot off. Anyone along the way asking about his uniform could be sweet talked out of ignoring it or dumped into a ditch along the road. The possibility he had lost Blackmun left him not caring about civilian casualties.

"You thinkin' it might be road agents, Colonel?"

"His mission was to secure weapons. It's more likely he was double crossed."

"If they had the guns we want, it'd be more valuable for them to sell to us," the sergeant said as he picked up the pace to match his commander's. "A pile of gold beats a handful of greenbacks."

Clark looked at the sergeant. The non-com knew more of Blackmun's mission than he should. While Clark hadn't insisted on it being kept secret, Blackmun hadn't had a chance to tell anyone else in the company the details. Giannini must have seen the captain stuff a handful of greenbacks into his pocket but not take any gold with him. All the soldiers knew of the need for cannon and heavier artillery. When they faced their first US Army unit, something more than sidearms and a few rifles were going to be needed.

They came out on the main road. Clark signalled for Giannini to release the riderless horse. How well Blackmun had trained the animal might now determine if he lived or died. He might be wounded and fighting to survive until reinforcements arrived, although Clark believed his captain to be dead. So much blood had soaked into the saddle no amount of elbow grease would ever polish it away.

"He was draped over the saddle, sir," said Giannini. "I've been thinking on that while we rode. Blackmun was tied across for quite a spell. If his throat was slit, he'd bleed out on the ground. If he was filled with bullets before getting tied down, the blood would drain into the leather."

"Sound reasoning, Sergeant." Clark believed the latter was most likely. Blackmun had flashed his wad of scrip and been killed for it. The killer might not have believed there was any gold to buy weapons, or perhaps there were never any weapons to sell. Gun runners were underhanded men who kept alive by being constantly suspicious and doubly treacherous.

They rode toward Denver, but Blackmun's horse veered northward before reaching the main road into town. Barely had they turned northward than the horse reared and pawed at the air.

"There he is, Colonel. In the brush."

Colonel Clark dismounted and went to Blackmun's body. The rope burns on his wrists showed how he had been lashed securely over his horse. Either he hadn't been all the way dead or had been tied down poorly and slipped off the horse. Clark rolled the captain onto his back.

"Five bullets. He was murdered." He drew out a knife and dug about in Blackmun's chest to find a piece of lead. It popped out. Clark wiped it off on the dead man's shirt and held it up.

"Looks to be a .44-40," Clark said.

"Cavalry? Winchester Model '73 carbines are what the cavalry use. At least in these parts." Giannini stood in the stirrups and looked around. "From the holes in his chest, he rode into an ambush and was shot down by a half dozen of them bluecoat varmints."

Clark cut out several more bullets. All were the same caliber. From the entry wounds, each rifleman had fired from a slightly different direction. Definitely Blackmun had been cut down in an ambush and never returned fire, though with his holster and six-shooters missing, that wasn't something he could verify.

"There, sir. In the road. Something shiny."

Clark dropped the bloody bullets and cleaned his knife on Blackmun's pants. He hiked to the spot Giannini pointed out, bent and picked up a brass button half buried in the dust.

"Cavalry," he confirmed.

"No telling when it might have been lost. This is the road to Fort Junction, the post up at the fork of Boulder and St Vrain Creeks. All it's been used for was guarding the Overland Stage route."

"Mail," Clark said. "Or perhaps it is a storage area for more." He tucked the button into his jacket pocket and mounted. "The button isn't tarnished enough to have lain there long." Clark turned his horse's face north toward the fort.

"What about the captain?"

"He's served well, but whatever mistake he made delivered him the fate he deserved." Clark never looked back as he galloped on.

Giannini's spat in Blackmun's direction, then followed his commander. They slowed when they saw a sign telling them they were a half dozen miles from Fort Junction. Clark pointed to a trail cutting to the east. They rode along until a river blocked their progress.

"This most likely is Boulder Creek," Giannini said. "I remember St Vrain being farther east.

Clark studied the sluggishly flowing creek for a minute

before saying, "The fort dumps its waste into this stream. We're not more than a few minutes' ride from finding a company of soldiers."

Cautioned to silence, Giannini rode behind the colonel until he received a signal to dismount. He pulled out his rifle and joined the officer. Clark already had a Winchester out. Together they silently crept up an embankment, then fell to their bellies.

"There's nothing but a sod wall around it," Clark said.

"I see breaks here and there. They haven't bothered maintaining it."

Clark squinted into the afternoon sun. Two sentry towers and a tall flagpole with the Stars and Stripes flapping in the brisk late afternoon breeze were the tallest structures.

"We can take out the sentries," Giannini said, sighting in on one tower.

"Hold your fire. We need to know more about the garrison." Clark began a slow infiltration and stopped when he reached a breach in the mud wall. He wiggled through, getting mud all over his uniform. His batman could clean off the filth.

Peering into the compound he counted soldiers drilling on the parade ground near the flagpole. Four mountain howitzers were lined up at the edge. Beyond the cannon a wooden structure housed two sentries making a slow circuit in opposite directions. From what Clark could see, this was the fort's armory. The entire time he watched no one entered. Beyond it were the stables. Both the freestanding armory and the way the buildings were situated kept him from counting mounts to estimate the fort's strength.

He shooed away a curious hen that came up to peck at him. Livestock of various kinds roamed freely inside the waist-high mud walls. He saw how settlers or soldiers could use those walls as a defensive bulwark against Indians. If another army unit attacked, Fort Junction would be overrun in a few minutes.

Backing off, he returned to Sergeant Giannini on the slope leading down into Boulder Creek.

"Any luck, Colonel?"

Clark outlined what he had seen. He took out his notebook and sketched the layout of the fort. Giannini added a few details, but Clark's reconnaissance provided the details necessary to raid the armory.

"What'll it be? A full-scale attack or do we let them send out a patrol before we attack?" Giannini sounded eager to get down to killing.

Clark scribbled notes.

"Both, Sergeant. We lure them out with an attack, then our main force cleans out their armory. I didn't see a wagon. We'll have to bring the one we used for transporting the gold from the train robbery."

"Will one be big enough? Rifle crates take up a lot more space than a few bars of gold."

"I'm putting you in charge of stealing a second wagon, Sergeant. For rifles, perhaps, for Gatling guns if they are stored here, for ammo and definitely shot, canister and 12-pound cannon balls to feed the howitzers." A feral grin twisted his lips. "Captain Blackmun did not die in vain. I hadn't intended to turn over any gold to those thieves, but they showed their true colors and gave us renewed resolve to avenge our fallen comrade."

"So they double crossed us first?"

Clark shot the sergeant a cold look, then rolled onto his belly and looked up at the flagpole. A shiny gold ball crested the pole. With his Whitfield the shot would have been easy. Using the shorter barreled Winchester made the target more difficult.

He got a good sight picture, then squeezed off a round.

The sun reflecting on the gold sphere, the wind and distance worked against him. He still sent his bullet ricocheting off into the distance when it grazed the gold top piece.

The sentries came awake and looked around, but colonel and sergeant were already making their way back to their camp to prepare for the AoA's first foray against a military force.

❧ 9 ❧

His body was found along the road into town," Allister Legende said. "The buzzards were enjoying a fine feast."

"Fine feast?" Frank Landry scoffed. "They were probably puking out their guts. He was rotten to the core."

"His name was Blackmun," said Legende. "From what little Mister Small found out about him, he was on the run from bounty hunters, though they were hardly chasing too aggressively."

"What? Why not?" Frank sipped at the glass of whiskey Legende furnished. He wanted to ask if it was one of his own bottles. He had lost track of his sample case when he'd taken out after Blackmun after leaving the Whore of Babylon Saloon. Whether serving him his own liquor was Legende's idea or something his butler thought was amusing remained to be seen. His dealings with Legende in the past had lacked a certain honesty. Stealing his samples would be minor compared to the accusations that had been bandied about years ago.

"The highest reward on his head was $50. All his wanted

posters stacked in a pile wouldn't bring a bounty hunter a hundred dollars. It seems he found his meal ticket with Clark."

"Now the worms have found their meal ticket in him," Frank said sourly. "I can't figure out a way of tracking back to Clark now that Blackmun's been killed."

"That thread is frayed, true," Legende said. "It's time to tug at the thread next to it in our tapestry."

"What do you mean?" Frank finished his whiskey and wondered if he should ask for another glass. Drowning his disappointment wasn't a good idea, but the whiskey was satisfying.

"Blackmun failed to convince the gunrunner of his honesty, if that ever can be accomplished in such illicit dealings. Let me put it this way. Blackmun failed to win the confidence of the gun dealer."

"He flashed a pile of money. The owlhoot decided it was better to take Blackmun's money and keep his guns for another sale. If he had any guns to sell. This might have been a confidence scheme."

"Lure shady men with money into an alley to rob them? While that's true, I think a better way to go is to believe the guns exist and that Blackmun failed to win over the sellers. You, Frank, are a born salesman. Sell yourself and let's look at the guns."

"What's that gain us? If those are soldiers selling Army weapons, they have nothing to do with Clark. We might catch them stealing government property, but we're no closer to stopping Clark."

"True, we bring other criminals to justice. While that's not a part of my assignment—*your* assignment—it accomplishes some good. Consider this. The deal goes through. Now, we have the guns. What do we do with them?" Legende

fixed his flame-filled eyes on Frank. The idea slowly perco-
lated up.

"We offer them to Clark, only instead of lying about
having weapons, we actually have a wagonload of them.
That's safer than the original plan, But what if he won't bite?"

"The story writes itself. We have the guns. Those soldiers
responsible are on trial. We can make it very public so Clark
cannot miss the news. That means we have a hot potato we
must toss in the air, only it will never cool. Who wants those
guns?"

"Clark intends to use them right away. He has to strike
before Colorado statehood is approved."

"Months. Weeks. He must strike quickly. He would see
our dilemma, being weighed down with guns no one else
wants and think he knows everything about the deal."

Frank nodded. He saw how Legende's plan came together.
The only problem was the added steps in the scheme. Find the
soldiers, arrest them, get word to Clark, it became more complicated than tracking Blackmun back to his camp and finding the
true strength arrayed against a newly minted state of Colorado.

"This can take some time," Frank said. He frowned.
"Emily might find out who's the traitor on Governor Routt's
staff first and get him to double cross Clark."

"Is that so bad?" Legende grinned. "You're afraid she will
beat you to Clark and his army?"

"I want this over. If she finds out everything first, more
power to her." Frank stared at his empty whiskey glass and
wanted another to get the foul taste of those words off his
tongue. "What's she found out so far? Going to all those
fancy parties must be wearing on her something fierce."

"She went to yet another of the governor's political rallies
last night. She hasn't reported what, if anything, she found."

"Is that something to worry about?"

Legende raised an eyebrow.

"Are you concerned for her, Frank? Would you shift your focus to being her assistant from finding which soldier is selling arms?"

"I'm not going to be in her shadow. She probably found someone to pump for information and hasn't bestirred her bones from a feather bed yet." Frank took out his pocket watch and made a point of studying it. He clicked shut the case and returned it to his vest pocket. "It's time for me to be out and about. However, I need enough flash money to convince the gun dealer I'm for real."

"But not so much he decides you, like Blackmun, can line his nest without need to actually part with the guns."

"I take that to mean the guns are still in Army control. If someone buys the guns from the soldiers, they will have to steal them."

"Noted. Once this is set in motion, I will see that the armory is placed under independent guard."

"A thousand dollars ought to be plenty," Frank said, naming the first amount that came to mind. He was willing to take far less. To his surprise Kingston came into the library carrying his silver tray. The pile of bills on it toppled as he held it out.

Frank kept his hand from shaking in anticipation as he took the money.

"I should have asked for more."

"If you need more, I can fetch it," Kingston said.

Frank looked at Legende, which the butler didn't. This was small change and not worth bothering the master over. He took the money and restrained the impulse to count it. Somehow, he knew there was exactly one thousand dollars here. Kingston had been waiting to bring it--he had been listening in for his cue. Frank looked around, wondering about the secret rooms and possibility of spy holes. He knew of Kingston and Mister Small. Who else counted Legende as their employer? There had been two bullets on the mantle indicating at least two unknown agents. Or was one of those Kingston's? That still meant one man went about his duties unknown and in secret.

Or was that another woman? Legende hadn't hesitated to add Emily's .45 derringer bullet to the others on the mantle.

"Mister Landry?"

"Sorry, I was guessing how much I'd need. This will be plenty, Kingston. Thanks."

The butler silently left. Legende stood and waited. Frank got the idea and also stood.

"I'll get to work. Can I count on Mister Small backing me up again?"

"Someone will be there, if Mister Small is not available. Good day, Mister Landry."

Frank ran his fingers over the stack of greenbacks and considered how far he could travel if he simply got on a stage and rode off. A thousand-dollar stake provided a powerful lot of cushion for whatever he did. But he needed his sample case.

And then there was Emily. He wasn't about to let her stop Clark. Determined to find the gunrunner, he left the Society HQ, mounted Barleycorn and returned to the Whore of Babylon. He didn't have long to wait.

"You want Gatlings?" A different man than the one who had met with Blackmun in the saloon bent close and whispered to Frank in a cracked voice. "You thinkin' on startin' a war?"

"What I want with those repeaters is my business." Frank slipped sideways in the chair so he could draw his Colt if the man showed the slightest hint of pulling a gun on him. The saloon was more crowded than when Blackmun and his contact had talked, but Frank doubted such mattered a hill of beans. Not to anyone in a place called the Whore of Babylon.

"Repeaters? You call them repeaters? Mister, they can shred an entire squad of soldiers. You fire four of them—you asked to buy four, right?—you can take on an entire company. They got what we call firepower."

"Who is 'we'?" Frank asked.

"Don't you worry none on that score. All you need to know is that we got the guns if you got the money."

"What else can you supply? Rifles?"

The man frowned, then nodded slowly and said, "Fifty Spencers. Fifty and ammunition. You want them *and* the Gatlings?"

Frank considered dropping mention of the howitzers into the mix, then decided that would scare the man off. Nobody who wasn't riding at the head of an army bought that kind of armament. Nobody who wasn't commanding an army or trying to sucker a crooked quartermaster into selling to a government agent.

"Let's take this real slow," Frank said. "Start with the rifles, then see about other items of interest." Frank read the man's expression well. "You want to sell as much as you can without going back to the well. That means when you steal the rifles, somebody'll notice. You won't have the chance to get the Gatlings later on."

"Don't go puttin' words in my mouth."

"Let me talk to your boss. He can decide how much of my gold he wants to haul off."

"Gold?" Greed flared on the man's face.

"This isn't a whim on the part of my superiors," Frank said. He waited a moment, then said in mock surprise, "You didn't think the guns were for my personal use, did you? The Comancheros ..." He let the sentence trail off. Let the soldier think he was going to sell guns to the Indians. "Let's powwow with your boss." Frank peeled a bill off the wad of greenbacks and dropped it on the table as he stood.

The hesitation made him worry he had overplayed his hand. Then the man got up and left the saloon, not even looking back. Frank followed him into the street. The man was already a couple buildings down in the mouth of the same alley where Blackmun had been waylaid. Frank sucked in a deep breath and let it out. The time had come to fish or cut bait.

"He's at the back of the alley," the man said.

"Is he higher in rank than a private?"

"Whatdya mean?" The man's hand went for his pistol. Frank grabbed his wrist and twisted hard to deter him from drawing.

"I mean you're a private. Or maybe you're a corporal?"

"Corporal," the man said, twisting free and rubbing his wrist. "How'd you guess?"

"Because he's not an idiot," came the cold words. "Not like you."

Frank sized up the newcomer fast. Here was someone used to giving commands and having them obeyed, but there wasn't the haughty arrogance that went with being an officer.

"What do I call you?" Frank held out his hand. "I'm Frank."

"Call me Sarge," the barrel-chested man said. He shot his corporal a dark look and turned away to march to the far end of the alley.

Frank was leery of letting the corporal follow him but went anyway. They stopped in a small alcove made from towering crates. Where the sergeant maneuvered Frank made a perfect trap. He was closed in by crates on three sides and faced both the non-coms.

"Money. Show me what you got." The sergeant held out his hand.

Frank pulled the greenbacks from his coat pocket with his left hand and held them out. As the sergeant grabbed, Frank let the bills scatter. At the same instant he whipped out his six-shooter and shoved it into the corporal's belly.

"The rifles. You're not stealing my money. Show me the rifles." He leaned a bit more and drove the steel barrel harder into the man's belly until he doubled over.

"We wouldn't do nuthin' like that, mister. Honest." The corporal stepped away from the punishing barrel in his gut.

"I would. Gimme the money." The voice boomed like the peal of doom.

The corporal turned and went for his six-gun. A tiny pop! was followed by the thunder of a six-shooter discharging in the enclosed space. The corporal had fired his six-shooter, but the slug tore into the ground. He pressed his hand over his heart, looked up in confusion, then died.

Frank fired past the sergeant's head. The passage of hot lead so close to the man's ear caused him to flinch away. Frank fired a couple more times. By the time he stepped out of the enclosure the sergeant had his gun out and trained on Frank.

"That wasn't one of your men double crossing you, was it?" Frank pointed with his still smoking pistol down the alley. The broad back of their assailant vanished as he cut back for the main street.

"Kinchloe's dead," the sergeant said, kneeling by the corporal. He looked up at Frank, sizing him up. "You shot him."

"The owlhoot trying to hold us up killed him."

The sergeant poked a finger into the bullet wound directly over Kinchloe's heart. He pushed Frank's Colt around, then looked back.

"You use a small caliber, but this is really small. Maybe a .22."

"I've got my Colt Navy chambered for .36 rounds." Frank

edged back to the alley and touched the brim of his hat with his pistol barrel. "Be seeing you in hell."

"Wait. Where are you going?"

"Bury your dead. I need to find somebody to sell me rifles who won't get robbed and shot."

"That wasn't any of my doing. Maybe Kinchloe got careless. You got the money?" The sergeant began gathering the dropped bills.

"I've got gold. That was only a down payment."

"What else do you want? Other than the rifles?" The sergeant crammed the scrip into his pocket. "We can deal. The more you want at one time, the better the price I can give you."

"Gatlings? The rifles and Gatling guns?" Frank considered how deep the hook was sunk. "And a howitzer. With gunpowder and cannon balls."

"Make me an offer for four mountain howitzers and all the rest."

Frank even helped the sergeant move the dead man to the street and heave him over his saddle. They rode out of Denver. Frank tried not to call out his thanks to Mister Small as they passed the man silently watching from across the street.

❧ 10 ❧

Emily O'Connor held up the page in the leather portfolio for enough light to read its contents. Governor Routt had locked it in his special drawer for a reason. She wanted to know what he already knew, and the first few lines excited her. He had an inkling that somebody on his staff had betrayed him but had not found out who.

"He doesn't know if he can trust any of his staff," she said softly. "He's certainly not the only one with such suspicions, and he doesn't even know Francis Marion Landry."

A sound from behind made her half turn in the chair. A strong hand under her chin pulled her head back. A gag was stuffed into her mouth and secured. She tried to claw at the hand but her attacker controlled her movement with the chin grip. Then a blindfold wrapped around her head.

For an instant she thought she had a chance. She grabbed his sleeve--a fancy cuff--and yanked hard enough to unbalance him. It also caused her to fall forward over the governor's desk. Pinned face down she was in no position to kick or claw. Her right arm was pulled around in a hammer lock.

Then her left joined it. A few quick turns of rope secured her hands.

She tried to scream, but the gag muffled her words. Worse, it lived up to its name and caused her to gag. The air was cut off to her lungs when the man pinched her nostrils shut. Her struggles quieted and then she slipped away, unconscious.

Whether it was an hour or an instant later, Emily tried to blink, but the blindfold still prevented her from so much as moving her eyes about. She heard chamber orchestra music in the distance. Then she was dragged down stairs, her feet bumping hard with every step. The impact almost made her pass out again. Frank had told her once how to escape from ropes, though how he knew was beyond her. As far as she could tell, he never had escaped from anything but their marriage.

But she tried going completely limp and turning her wrists. Hope flared when the ropes loosened just a little. She worked on the slack, but being dragged along like a sack of potatoes prevented her from effectively pulling free. A sudden gust of cold air brought her out of her semi-coma.

Outside!

She was being kidnapped and taken away from the governor's party. The more people around her the better chance she had of being seen and her abductor stopped. A convulsive twist freed her from the man's grasp. She landed hard on a flagstone and scraped her arms. Again she tried to scream for help. Rubbing her face against the rough stone, hoping to pull the gag from her mouth failed. The man grunted as he hoisted her upright, then threw her over his shoulder rather than dragging her further.

This let her kick and wiggle. He was too strong for her to have any effect. The sounds of the party faded away. A door creaked open, then slammed shut. Seconds later she crashed down onto a hard seat that bounced like she was on a spring.

The kidnapper muttered constantly as he moved her around. More ropes fastened her securely. Emily rocked forward and back. The seat gave under her and bobbed about. Exhausted she settled down and tried to figure out what had happened to her. The abduction was obvious enough. Someone had managed to sneak up behind her, though how he had done that without coming in the main entrance was a mystery. He couldn't have followed her aerial route jumping from balcony to balcony.

He was already in the office. The shadows had hidden him. She must have interrupted him before he could find what she had so quickly. That decided, she tried to free herself from her bonds.

The only thing she determined was the man knew how to tie a secure knot. Even with the slack in the ropes around her wrists, she wasn't able to get free. As she moved, the bouncing motion hinted that she had been tied to a carriage seat—but the seat wasn't in a carriage.

A carriage house. The governor's carriage house and this seat was being repaired. Or stored.

Emily was satisfied she had deduced everything that had happened to her, but it did nothing to free her from her predicament. She was too firmly tied. All she could do was wait to see what her kidnapper did with her.

She shuddered at the thoughts her fevered imagination concocted.

Those imaginings caused her to thrash about, but this only raised clouds of dust. Her nose twitched and when she sneezed, she almost choked to death. Emily changed tactics and tried to catch the blindfold on a sharp edge and work it off. Nothing worked. Tired both physically and emotionally, she sagged.

She came immediately alert when the creaking door sounded again and a gust of cold air blew against her sweat-stained bodice and face. Emily tried to call out.

The man who had entered cried something she didn't understand, then a shot deafened her. The closed space made it echo endlessly. Before her hearing returned to normal, the blindfold was ripped from her eyes and fingers fumbled to get the gag out of her mouth.

She blinked at Paul Vandenberg, standing over her with a smoking pistol in his hand.

"Are you all right? Did that fiend do anything to you?"

Emily strained to look past Vandenberg. On the dusty floor sprawled a man, face down.

"Who is it? Was it?" she amended. The bindings fell from her wrists.

"You were almost free. Your wrists are scraped up and burned a little from the rope, but you could have gotten free in another few minutes."

She grabbed Paul Vandenberg by the shoulders and pulled herself to her feet. Her legs threatened to betray her, but his strong arm around her waist supported her. Emily stood on tiptoe to see over his shoulder.

"Who *was* it?"

"He won't bother you anymore. It was Lucius."

"Who?" Emily pried herself free and went to the fallen man. He was dressed in evening wear. She turned his head enough to see. "This is the governor's personal secretary!"

"I would never have thought Lucius was capable of such ... such terrible deeds." Vandenberg tried to take her in his arms again, but Emily avoided his grasp. A half dozen men came from the house at a dead run and crowded into the carriage house.

"What's going on? I demand to know!" Governor Routt looked from Emily to Vandenberg and only then at the dead man. A small man wearing a waiter's uniform whispered in the governor's ear. Routt nodded, then said, "You both come with me back to the mansion. I must hear everything."

"Miss O'Connor has had a frightening experience, Governor. Can't it wait until she's regained her senses?"

"Thank you, Mister Vandenberg, but I am quite capable of telling everything that has happened. Have the police been called, sir?" She danced around Vandenberg's grasp again. "It will save time if I tell my story to them and you at the same time."

Emily saw how the waiter once more commanded the governor's attention. They huddled in argument, then Routt lost the argument.

"Please, Miss O'Connor, let's go to the house. It ... this ... you present a problem for not only me but the entire statehood movement."

Emily started to blurt out that political considerations should be secondary to criminal ones, but she found herself guided from the carriage house, Paul Vandenberg on one elbow and the waiter on the other. Vandenberg won the silent tug of war for her and the waiter hurried on to speak to the governor all the way into the house.

It didn't take a mental giant to realize the waiter was something more than a simple server. Emily wasn't sure but thought she saw a small pistol tucked into the waiter's cummerbund. He was some sort of security guard. They went up the backstairs. Emily worried they would go into the governor's office where she'd have to explain why she had rifled through his papers, but they continued along the corridor and finally entered the room from which she had balcony-jumped to the office.

"Please, Miss O'Connor, have a seat." The governor pointed to one so she had a view out the window into the breaking dawn. Emily settled down. Once she did, exhaustion

swept over her. She had been through too much for one
night.

The governor sat opposite her, so his face was partially
hidden in shadow. The waiter stood behind him and Paul
Vandenberg sank into a chair to her right. He moved it so he
was turned more in her direction than in the governor's. To
her way of thinking, this put him on Routt's side and not on
hers.

"Thank you, Mister Vandenberg, for rescuing me. How
did you happen to realize I had been kidnapped?" She spoke
before the governor could start his own interrogation. She
wanted to avoid answering questions about the ribbon-tied
folder and the information about Colonel Clark in the documents she had seen.

"I wondered where you had gone. Horace and Clarissa
Toms had left and I saw Lucius skulking about, going
upstairs. I followed but couldn't find him. I returned to the
party but became curious and searched the grounds. I saw
him and, well, the rest you know."

"How is it you're carrying a pistol?" The waiter asked the
question Emily wanted answered.

"It certainly saved my life, but you weren't planning on
using it at Governor Routt's soiree, were you, Paul?" She
smiled winningly. Emotions flowed across his face in such a
flood she couldn't separate them.

"I came through dangerous parts of town to the
mansion," he said. To Emily's ears, that didn't ring true.

"Lucky for the young lady," the waiter said. "Why'd Lucius
want to snatch you like he did, Miss O'Connor?"

"Could I get a glass of water?" She locked eyes with the
waiter. Not a muscle twitched to honor her request. His
training wasn't in serving others, at least not for food or
drink.

"I'll get it, Emily." Vandenberg sprang up to fill a glass

from a pitcher on a table. He poured one for the governor, too.

"You have guessed Mister Burlington is not on my serving staff." Governor Routt looked uneasy at the confession.

"A Pinkerton?" She tried not to sound too sure of herself, but she had encountered scores of Pinks. This Burlington fellow had the attitude she had seen in many of those agents hired out as bodyguards.

The fake waiter's eyebrows rose. He started to speak, the clamped his mouth shut.

Governor Routt smiled and said, "I've noticed she is a keen observer, sir. Is this why Lucius took you prisoner the way he did?"

"I have no idea who he is. Was. From your comments, he was on your staff. In what capacity?" She knew already, but hearing the answers Routt was willing to give gave new information.

"He was my personal secretary." Routt's smile faded. "He was my trusted personal secretary. I thought I could count on him."

"Sir, should you discuss this any more in front of her?" Burlington glared at Emily. She smiled sweetly.

"About the attempt to prevent Colorado from becoming a state? Is that what you mean, sir?" She took small pleasure in poking and prodding the Pinkerton agent. A private conversation between her and the governor would be more to her liking, but the Pink and Paul Vandenberg made no move to leave.

"I am surprised you know of such things, Miss O'Connor. Since you seem to, yes, that is it. There has been vital information leaked from my office. It pains me that Lucius was responsible."

"I've taken care of that, albeit inadvertently," Vandenberg said.

"So you have, Paul. I wish you hadn't killed him. Finding what he knew would have been useful."

"Have you hired an army of Pinkertons to oppose Colonel Clark?" She looked from Burlington to the governor and tried to catch Vandenberg's reaction from the corner of her eye.

"We hope to head off such a massive event," Routt said. He wasn't surprised that she knew so much about Clark and his ambitions. She gave him credit for not thinking she was an empty-headed piece of feminine fluff and assumed she was a significant player in this deadly game.

"I'll stop this Clark fellow before he can raise an army. Otherwise, the US Army will take care of him." Burlington took a step closer. "What do you know, Miss O'Connor? Everything. You haven't begun to spill the extent of your meddling in this."

"What is your involvement, Paul? Other than being so heroic and rescuing me?" She batted her eyelashes at him and graced him with a warm smile. Most men melted under such attention. Paul Vandenberg was no exception. The look on his face changed as he switched to a political manner.

The way Vandenberg responded so carefully told her he had a speech memorized for this precise moment, whether she or the governor or someone else posed the question. He launched into how he sought Governor Routt's election as first state governor, some political items that passed over her head and then, "I will be happy to take over Lucius' duties, Governor. I am sure Horace can do without my services."

"I don't understand, Paul. You work for Horace Toms? And for Governor Routt?" Emily sipped at her water, looking over the rim of the glass.

"I suppose what I do is best described as liaison between the railroad and the territorial government."

Emily had no idea what that meant, other than Vandenberg moved from the political to the financial centers of the territory without anyone questioning him.

"You are ever so important, Paul," she said. "Can you give up such a fine job with Mister Toms?" The real question she wanted to ask was if Vandenberg intended to give up the railroad owner's wife in exchange for political influence.

"It's not a sacrifice, Emily. It's my civic duty. If Governor Routt will accept me as Lucius' replacement. I am privy to much of his dealings already. Learning the rest of the job would take less time for me than anyone else brought in cold." He looked ill at ease, as if he realized how lame that sounded, but the governor was nodding. He whispered to Burlington, then stood.

"I'll be honored to have you on my office staff, Paul. Now, I must get some sleep. My apologies again for this unfortunate night, Miss O'Connor. We must discuss matters at greater length when we are both rested."

As the governor passed by her, Emily shot to her feet and tugged at his sleeve. She whispered, "Did you have the combination to the safe? On the train where Clark stole the gold?"

"What? No, of course not. That's entirely a security matter for Horace. Good evening, Miss. Or should I say good morning?" The governor left, Burlington moving to cut Emily off from asking any further questions.

Paul Vandenberg came up behind her and put his hands on her shoulders.

"You're shaking, Emily. John is right. You need to rest."

"John? Oh, Governor Routt. Yes, it has been trying." She pressed her hand against her skirt and felt the derringer in a pocket. The weapon had done her no good once she was trussed up, blindfolded and gagged. The only positive thing she saw was that she had not been forced to kill a man as Vandenberg had so conveniently done. Lucius wasn't going to spill his guts about involvement with Clark with a bullet in the back of his head.

"I'll see you home."

"You're such a gentleman, Paul. I suppose I need to make an appointment to see the governor by asking your permission now. What a fine job that must be, personal secretary to man who will be the state's first governor."

"I like to think of it as him being Colorado territory's last governor," he said.

"Yes, out with the old, in with the new. Only they are both the same. Isn't that so?" Not for the first time she wished she could play poker with Vandenberg. Reading his thoughts was far too easy.

❦ 11 ❦

W e're being watched." Frank Landry rested his hand on the Colt Navy but didn't draw. He and Mister Small had ridden from Denver before dawn. The sky was barely pink with the fingers of a new day and already he doubted this would be a good day.

"No one is watching," the giant of a man said.

"Are the gold coins buried?" Frank kicked at a pile of brush. A rawhide thong poked out from beneath. If he dug further, he'd find a canvas bag loaded with double eagles. There were three more hidden around the area according to a pattern Allister Legende had chosen.

Frank didn't kid himself. Legende wanted the gold hidden this way so if his two agents died, there'd be a chance of recovering the coins. Agreeing to the sergeant's order where to meet had its drawbacks. This was likely a trap intended to kill whomever had the gold. Still, no other way of getting past the crooked quartermaster and casting out bait to reel in Colonel Clark looked likely. While Legende had never said, Frank thought the man had made a request of the Army to borrow the rifles and had been turned down.

At least Legende hadn't turned over the sergeant to his superiors. Doing that ended the plan to snare Clark before he sent his militia whooping and hollering into Denver to seize power and declare himself king of Auraria. Or whatever highfalutin title he had picked for himself.

"He'll wonder why there's not a wagon for the rifles." Frank worried over a hundred details that would scotch the deal.

"He has to bring them. There'll be a wagon. Why'd he want to keep it when he intends to take the gold and ride away to keep from being arrested?"

"Arrested and court-martialed," Frank said. "The Army will stand him in front of a firing squad ten seconds after they find out about his gunrunning. They'd do that, wouldn't they, rather than hang him?"

He spoke to empty air. A quick spin failed to give even a hint where Mister Small had gone. But he heard hoofbeats approaching from the direction of Fort Junction. A quick, instinctive move smoothed wrinkles in his coat. He struck a pose, left thumb hooked under his lapel and right foot forward. Like an actor on stage, he prepared his speech as he had done a thousand times before. Then he had sold whiskey to reluctant saloon owners. Now he had to buy rifles. And Gatling guns and howitzers. From traitors prepared to cut him down if he made a single misstep.

Or, considering how they operated, even if he did everything exactly right.

The sergeant galloped up and came to a fast halt. His horse kicked up a choking dust cloud. Frank moved away to keep the soldier in view in case he wanted to hide treachery behind that brown, dusty veil. The man jumped to the ground and stomped over.

"You got the gold?" the sergeant demanded belligerently.

Frank chose to answer with just a note of boredom at such

an attitude. Being cowed now weakened his bargaining position.

"Do you have the weapons? I don't see them. I don't even see a wagon loaded with what I'm buying." Frank read the sergeant's uneasiness as worry and not betrayal. "Something's gone wrong? Why don't you have the goods?"

"I can't get the cannons or Gatlings, just the rifles." The sergeant's earlier demeanor had been bravado and nothing more. Frank saw the opening and dug into it.

"And ammunition, bullets and anything else that comes with a brand new Spencer?"

"Look, there's an uprising down around Creede. The whole fort's buzzing about that. The rifles are being loaded onto a wagon right now and will come past in a few minutes. The driver and guards are all my men. You give me the gold and you ride off in the wagon with the goods."

"How many rifles?"

"Fifty."

Frank heard the lie. He waved his hand to show the deal was off. If the sergeant's story about an Indian uprising at Creede was true, the Army and any recruited local militia there needing rifles, he was in a pickle.

"All right," the sergeant said reluctantly. "I can deliver twenty rifles. Give me a thousand in gold and--"

"Two hundred. Ten dollars a rifle and not a plugged nickel more." Frank saw desperation in the man's eyes. The sergeant either took what was offered and hightailed it or stayed in the Army and fought Indians in the Powderhorn Wilderness. If Frank sized up the non-com properly, the sergeant had brought down the wrath of his superiors for some offense and was going to be cashiered. Stealing the rifles gave him a few dollars and revenge for his treatment.

"I got four men to pay."

"Is that a problem?" Frank knew it wasn't. The sergeant

might split the gold with one or two of the others, but there would be fewer soldiers before the sun made its way up over the horizon, thanks to a deadly double cross.

"Show me the gold or I tell them to keep on driving, and I'll take care of you myself."

Frank went to the bush and kicked it away from the shallow hole. The sergeant pounced on the gold like a wolf on a lamb. He ripped open the drawstring and ran his fingers through the coins. When he looked up, the image of a wolf burned itself even more vividly into Frank's head.

"The wagon'll be along any time now," the sergeant said. He stood, the leather pouch clutched in both hands as if it might grow wings and fly away.

Distant gunfire made Frank turn and look up the road in the direction of the fort.

"What's going on?" Frank slid his six-shooter from the holster and cocked it. The sergeant paid him no attention.

"Something's wrong," the soldier said. "Nobody's supposed to do any shooting. They loaded the rifles and were heading out a few minutes after me. I swear."

"Drop the gold. You can get it when I see the rifles." Frank was surprised that the sergeant obeyed so quickly. He tied off the pouch and dropped it back into the shallow hole. A kick covered it with dirt. The sergeant took three quick steps and vaulted into the saddle. In seconds he galloped out of sight.

Frank grabbed Barleycorn's reins and stepped up. For a moment, he sat astride his gelding, considering what to do. The smart thing was to ride hellbent for leather back to Denver. Instead, he followed the sergeant. Mister Small could keep up or report to Legende. All that mattered to Frank was getting the rifles to use as bait for Colonel Clark.

The closer he got to the fort, the louder and more frequent came the gunfire. He almost wheeled about and rode away when he heard the distinctive whap-whap-whap of a Gatling gun cutting loose its leaden storm. Whatever went down, the soldiers returned fire with their heavy automatic weapons. He expected to hear the cannon firing. If the uprising at Creede had spread this far north and on the eastern slope of the Front Range, a mountain howitzer would end the attack fast.

But if Indians attacked, why take on Fort Junction? This was an Army stronghold in comparison to the softer underbelly of stagecoach routes, railroad shipments and the constant flow of freight wagons over the mountains to the gold fields around Georgetown and farther south toward Central City.

"I've got to get into the fort," the sergeant said.

Frank jerked around. He had halted beside the soldier and hadn't noticed. The earsplitting reports and rising white gunsmoke from the fort just over a rise in the road held his attention and made him careless. He was no stranger to gunfights, but it had been a spell since he had seen a battle of these proportions. Rather than slackening, the tumult increased.

"Wait," Frank called. Too late. The soldier pulled his carbine from the saddle sheath, jacked in a round and lit out. He topped the rise and disappeared.

As foolish as could be, Frank rode after the soldier. He came to a spot in the road with a better look at Fort Junction and tried to make sense of what he saw. The dirt wall on the western side had been trampled by a cavalry assault. Once the worthless wall was breached, men flooded into the compound and fanned out.

Two soldiers had pried open the door to the armory and had wheeled out a Gatling gun. They swung it back and forth, cutting through their attackers' ranks, but Frank saw they were losing the battle. Too many men opposed them.

He started to call out when a man on the roof of the arsenal moved to attack the soldiers in front of the armory. The outlaw stood behind the Gatling gun crew and opened fire with a six-shooter. Both soldiers died. Their attacker stood upright, thrust his gun high in the air and let out a blood curdling cry of victory.

The fight went against the soldiers fast after that. Frank tugged on his horse's reins to get away from the carnage.

He froze when he found himself peering down the barrel of a rifle. The man sighted in on him, and at this range could never miss.

T he men are antsy, Colonel." Lieutenant Zamora picked his teeth with a thick-bladed knife. When he finished his dental cleaning, he shoved the knife back into a sheath at his side.

Clark glared at his new second in command and considered disciplining him for such a breach of decorum. Then he pushed it aside. The attack mattered more, and Zamora was one of the few soldiers in the Army of Auraria who had actual combat experience. Sergeant Giannini hinted at being in a few battles, but Clark wondered about his honesty in this matter. Giannini talked a good fight, but when they had attacked the train to seize the treasury for the new nation, he had been nowhere to be seen. He might have been picking off the other outlaw gang as he claimed. Clark questioned it.

Corporal Antrim shifted nervously in his saddle next to his leader. He tapped his fingers on his belt buckle, keeping his hand inches from his holstered pistol. The company behind him muttered in low voices, but all together they caused quite a ruckus.

"Sergeant, quiet the men. We are only a mile from the

fort." Clark twisted the map to catch as much starlight as possible to read it. It was both a boon and a hindrance that they struck during the dark of the moon. His untrained soldiers could use the brilliant, silvery light to better fight, but the darkness kept the Army sentries from seeing them as they advanced.

Such it was in any battle. Good and bad. A decent commander made the best of what was always a dangerous situation.

"The men're wondering if we fight to avenge Blackmun or if there's something more," Zamora said. "They'd fight better if they thought they could loot." Zamora spat onto the ground. Curiously, the spittle caught the starlight and seemed to glow with its own inner diamond light. "No sense telling them raping ain't gonna happen. No women."

"They could have at the dead soldiers and the mules. I hear tell how Army mules are--" Antrim stopped talking as Clark drew his pistol and cocked it. His batman mumbled an apology.

Clark lowered the six-gun's hammer and laid his hand across the saddle in front of him.

"You talk to the men. What will motivate them best?"

"Most of 'em just want to kill something. A few of the boys have been kicked out the Army. Revenge is good enough for them. Too many don't know why we're here."

"Ten dollars to every man who claims a Gatling. Twenty for a captured howitzer."

"In gold?" Zamora became more animated at the notion of such a generous reward.

"In gold. And you, Lieutenant, you do well and you can win a promotion to captain."

"That and a nickle buys me a flat beer in Denver."

"The higher the battlefield rank, Lieutenant, the greater your authority in the new nation. Captain Blackmun had been promised a governorship down south. That post has yet to be filled now that he died."

"You'd put me in charge of a country?"

"I call them provinces. You have seen the map of Colorado Territory. A province including Ouray and the silver mines in the southwest would be valuable to the proper man."

"Governor Chuy Zamora. I like the sound of that."

"Then muster the men, form the ranks and let's capture the weapons we'll need to prevent statehood and give us Auraria!" Clark saw that his lieutenant was properly motivated. He turned to his batman. Corporal Antrim still tapped out a tattoo on his belt buckle. "And you, Antrim, you are in line for a promotion to sergeant."

"What about him?" Antrim pointed to Giannini. The sergeant argued with two men on foot.

"I have other plans for him, Corporal."

"Make that sergeant, Colonel. I like the sound of it. Sergeant Antrim. Are we ready to grab them guns?"

Clark raised the hand holding his pistol, cocked and fired. The foot-long orange and blue flame lit the predawn with eye-dazzling color. All around he heard a collective intake of breath, then Zamora let out a chilling cry. The Army of Auraria surged forward.

Clark put his heels to Bucephalus' flanks. Even the powerful stallion had trouble keeping up with the front wave of the attack on Fort Junction.

The stallion cleared the mud wall and landed hard inside the parade ground. Clark turned first left and then right, firing as he rode. He cared less about his bullets taking out the half-asleep soldiers trying to defend the fort than sowing chaos. The flood of his militia--the Army of Auraria!--pushed the soldiers back.

Then the slaughter began. He had ordered his troops to

kill everyone. No surrender, no quarter. Clark spun around, Bucephalus rearing and pawing at the air.

"Bugler!" he bellowed. "Sound the orders. Deguello!" No quarter. Ever. If he left even one soldier behind, his plans would be jeopardized. Let the Army puzzle over how the attack came about and who won the day. The longer it took their investigators, the easier it would be for him to lead the AoA into Denver and seize power before the statehood documents were signed. Before, the US Army might show reluctance in defending a mere territory. After the ink dried, the full force of a Federal army victorious against the South would be launched to crush him.

"Forward! Don't hold back!"

He shouted himself hoarse, and then his orders were drowned out by the bull fiddle roar of a Gatling gun. Bullets ripped past him and caused his stallion to bolt. Clark clung to the saddle horn and fought to regain control. The horse had other ideas.

The headlong rush proved to Clark's benefit. He charged out of control toward the commanding officer's quarters. He gave up trying to regain dominance over Bucephalus and fired wildly at the major emerging half dressed and holding his saber in his hand. One of Clark's bullets hit the saber blade and ricocheted off. The impact staggered the officer.

Clark kicked free of his horse and landed atop the major. The impact knocked the wind from him, but it knocked out the commanding officer. Clark lay flat on his back, eyes staring up into the dawn-lit sky.

Gasping, chest hurting like a million demons infested him, Clark struggled to his feet. His legs almost betrayed him as pain shot up from his long-ago injured thigh. The Gatling still chattered away, then went silent. He rubbed his eyes to clear them. One of his men had climbed to the roof of the free standing armory and had gunned down the Gatling crew from behind. In celebration, the AoA soldier threw his hands up high and fired into the air.

Clark regained his breath in time to see the victor die. A soldier had taken an easy shot to rob the AoA of its first obvious hero. Clark grabbed the major's sword and waved it about. His bullet had broken off the tip. He never noticed as he ran forward, seeing red. A slash to the left, another to the right and then he reached the marksman who had killed the hero who had taken out the Gatling gun crew.

"Die!" Clark raised the saber high and brought it slashing down. The edge was dull but the blade carried heft. It smashed into the rifleman's shoulder. The impact vibrated all the way up Clark's arm and caused him to stumble away.

He would have died then and there if Corporal Antrim hadn't rushed up, a six-shooter in each hand. Both guns blazed away and saved Clark from a soldier training his rifle on the colonel.

"I saw you jump their commander," Antrim said. "That was about the bravest thing I ever did see in all my born days."

"My horse. Bucephalus. Fetch my horse. And a gun. I need a gun." Clark took one of Antrim's pistols as it was shoved into his hand. He walked about in a daze and hardly realized when he stepped up and once more sat astride his stallion.

Rather than the carnage around him, he stared out to the rise some distance from the fort. That road led to Denver.

He saw a flash as a gun discharged, but the roar all around him drowned out any report from the distant gunfire. Whatever happened there meant nothing.

Fort Junction had fallen. To him. To the now-battle blooded Army of Auraria!

"Wagons. Lieutenant Zamora! Load wagons with everything in the armory. Sergeant Giannini. Harness the mules to the caissons. Get the cannons rolling out of here. Victory is ours! Victory for the Nation of Auraria!"

It took less than twenty minutes before Colonel Clark led his troops in triumph, leaving behind blood-soaked ground and almost a hundred corpses.

The war of liberation had begun!

❧ 13 ❧

Colonel Clark's lookout took aim. Frank Landry stared straight down the barrel. It wasn't a large caliber rifle, but he felt as if he could reach down the length with his arm and touch the bullet waiting to come searing out into his head.

He started for his Colt Navy when the muzzle flash and report blinded and deafened him. Barleycorn tried to bolt and run, but Frank Landry held the horse firmly under rein. He did that because he was still alive. Beyond the man sprawled facedown on the ground Mister Small tucked away his deadly Colt New Line. It was only a .22, but it proved deadly in the hands--the immense hands--of a skilled marksman.

"He's a goner," Mister Small said. "I shot him in the back of the head."

"I owe you a bottle from my whiskey case. What's your pleasure?"

"I don't drink."

Frank stared at the man in amazement. Mister Small was

so tall his head came to Frank's mid chest although he sat astride his horse.

"It's just as well. I don't have enough in my sample case to get a gent your size drunk."

The gunfire from the fort slowed to a few occasional shots. Then all that remained were the piteous moans of dying men. Frank was glad he didn't have field glasses to study the killing scene under magnification. The new day's light shone down on too many men who would never see another noon.

"Clark's men," he said. "This is one of them and the rest are down there. Who else could it be? They're stealing the armaments now."

"What do you want me to do?" Mister Small finished searching the man he'd cut down and had removed a few coins from his pocket and two sweat-stained scraps of paper. He tucked those into a vest pocket.

"Ride back to Denver and tell Legende everything that's happened. I'll keep on the trail to find where they're taking the cannon and other guns."

"Will you attack when you find their hideout?"

Frank held out his hand. He had been shivering a few seconds before at the closeness of being gunned down. But not now. He felt up to the chore of trailing the newly formed wagon train and keeping an eye on Colonel Clark.

"I'll get word to you as quick as a fox," he promised. There wasn't any way in hell he'd attack an entire encampment of well-armed men who had shown no mercy in their attack.

Mister Small nodded once, then stepped back into shadow. Frank started to call out. He had a further message, but this was for Emily. He would find the heart of the rebellion before she did. But Mister Small had disappeared.

The clatter and creak of wagons, caissons and artillery

carriages rolling away distracted him. Clark led his men directly west. Frank tried to remember the terrain, but he was more accustomed to prowling the city streets of Denver, bar hopping in an attempt to sell just one more case of whiskey. While no stranger to the frontier and its high lonesome, he had learned over the years a smoky saloon or a young lady's boudoir were more to his liking.

The column with the stolen guns vanished around a bend in the road. Frank waited a few more minutes, then rode to the fort. There might be survivors. He entered through a long section of broken mud fence. Barleycorn stepped almost daintily to keep from tromping on dead bodies. They hadn't been shot that long ago, but the stench was already enough to gag a maggot. Frank pulled out his pocket handkerchief and tied it around his nose. This helped some, but the rising foulness was almost more than he could bear.

He rode a pattern crisscrossing the parade ground, going from one wall to the one directly across, then changing direction to hunt for more wounded. Clark's men were nothing if not efficient.

"Savage is a better description than efficient." He found several soldiers who had been scalped. Others had been gutted. He rode past the armory. The doors had been ripped off and only a few weapons remained inside, racked and ready for soldiers who would never have a need for them. The Gatling crew shot from behind had been strung up to look like scarecrows.

Frank looked away and rode toward the commanding officer's office. Along the way he halted and stared at the body on the ground.

"You didn't sell me the guns quick enough, Sergeant. If you had there wouldn't have been any reason for Clark to destroy the post." Then he realized that wasn't a big concern for the filibusterer. He had killed everyone and taken what he wanted. If the guns hadn't been in the armory, Clark would have still killed everyone. The only way the sergeant would have survived was to take Frank's money and ride like the wind, no matter the direction.

He walked Barleycorn to the HQ and dismounted. The horse began to jerk nervously at the reins. Frank didn't fault the gelding for such nervousness. The stench was rising along with the sun and the buzz of flies was deafening. He looked into the sky and saw dozens of dark specks swinging about in wide circles. Buzzards waiting to see if it was safe to dine on the banquet laid out for them. Across the grounds he saw four-legged carrion eaters invading the compound to steal from the circling vultures.

He went into the commanding officer's office and looked around. A map nailed on the wall showed the terrain for the upper half of Colorado. Fort Junction had been marked with a red X. From here he studied trails and roads to the west. If he were Clark, his base camp wouldn't be to the north. Instead, it was in the hills to the south and on the east side of the Front Range. The rugged terrain and lack of settlements afforded hundreds of places to bivouac a large militia.

Frank tore the map from the wall since the soldiers wouldn't need it anymore. He tucked it under his vest and stepped back onto the porch outside the office. A spasm almost made him lose what food he had in his stomach. The scene before had been terrible. Now it was something not even Dante could have invented.

"A new circle of Hell," Frank decided. Once more, he hunted among the gore and body parts now being fought over by coyotes and buzzards for any sign of human life.

Nothing.

He swung into the saddle and rode through the gap in the dirt fence, going west. The sun behind him showed the deep ruts left by the wagons and caissons, but the artillery pieces cut the deepest ruts since their carriage wheels were the narrowest. Frank came to a fork in the road within a half mile.

"Now to see how smart I am."

The T branch went due north and another straight south. He was pleased to see his guess was born out. The caravan had headed south. A snap of the reins got his gelding moving. Within a half hour, the smell of death on his clothes from simply riding into Fort Junction faded. At least he couldn't smell it any longer. Barleycorn still seemed skittish.

Frank stopped occasionally when he saw streams running down to Boulder Creek to let his horse drink. He did his best to wash off his hands, face and coat, but the horse still nervously pawed the ground and made riding a chore.

The reason for the gelding's unease hit him at the same time he spotted a solitary rider in the road ahead. He drew rein to hang back. Clark had posted a rear guard and the man had to be drenched in blood. That made Barleycorn shy.

The guard might not have seen Frank, but he heard the horse whinnying. A single look over his shoulder made him bend forward and begin whipping his horse with the reins. Not thinking, Frank gave chase. The guard sought to overtake the column to warn of pursuit. The only lucky break Frank caught was the lookout not drawing his six-shooter and firing into the air to signal the others.

Barleycorn showed more stamina and, in the end, more speed. Frank overtook the guard. A lariat bounced at his knee, but he had never worked as a cowboy, at least not long enough to learn to expertly rope and hogtie. Head down, he urged his horse to even more speed. Barleycorn gave him just a mite more so they galloped side by side.

It was an easy shot from here for Frank. His Colt rode in a cross-draw holster. When he slipped it free it was already pointed in the right direction. But he no more wanted to alert Clark's army than he did to end up like the sergeant back at the fort.

With a loud yell, he launched himself. Clawing, flailing, he grabbed for the other rider. The man tried to veer away, but Frank caught a handful of his faded green shirt. Cloth ripped as Frank fell, but his weight and the strength of the cloth were enough to unseat the man. They crashed to the ground.

Frank had a split second to realize what was to come. The rider had been taken by surprise. This was all it took for Frank to recover, come to his knees and draw his six-shooter. Clark's soldier moaned and writhed about on the ground.

"Move and I'll drill you. I swear I will." Frank got to his feet and took the time to regain his balance. His six-gun never wavered as he pointed it at the fallen rider.

"What's it you want? You got no right!"

"You with the Nation of Auraria?" Frank plucked the man's pistol from his belt and shoved it under his own. A second gun came in handy if he had to shoot it out.

"What's that? Oh, that's what the colonel calls his country." The man rose painfully, half bent over and holding his back. "I swear you busted bones inside me. Why'd you go and do that?" Then he looked up, confused. "You lookin' to join up? In our army?"

Before Frank could answer, the whine of a bullet tore through the air not an inch from his ear. The man offering him a position in the rebel army stiffened, his eyes rolled up and he toppled like a felled tree. Shaking off his shock, Frank knelt and whirled about. Three riders galloped hard for him, their guns blazing. One had a rifle. Frank thought this was the one who killed the man beside him. The other two threw lead from pistols with no accuracy at all. The range was too great for them to be effective.

He grabbed for his horse's reins, but the frightened gelding lit out like its tail was on fire, leaving him alone to face the three killers. No doubt in his mind remained that they were fresh from the slaughter when the one in the lead shouted, "For the new nation. For Colonel Clark!"

Frank steadied his gun hand and began firing. The range was too much for him, too. But to his surprise one of the pistol wielders jerked to the side and fell from his horse. He hit the ground and didn't stir a muscle.

Frank looked at the six-shooter in his hand. That was a fabulous shot. Lucky, but he'd take it. When it came up empty, he thrust it into his holster and drew the pistol he had taken as a spare.

It took him a few seconds to realize both the attacking riders were dodging lead his pistol didn't send their way. The one with the rifle fell from his horse, but he kicked about in the dirt and scrambled to find cover in a nearby gulley. This left a single rider with a six-gun.

Frank never knew what possessed him. He started walking forward at a steady pace, firing every time his right foot touched ground. It was a slow motion frontal assault that shouldn't have worked. But it did. One slug tore through the man's right arm. His six-shooter fell from nerveless fingers. As he turned to retreat, another rifle report sounded. The rider threw up his arms and tumbled from horseback.

With some disdain, Frank tossed aside his now empty six-gun, drew his Colt Navy and began reloading, oblivious to the bullets sailing past him. When he once more had six cartridges in the cylinder, he started walking toward the rifleman in the ditch.

"No, wait. I give up!" The man threw aside his rifle and raised his hands. That was the last thing he ever did. An accurate bullet hit him in the side of the head, knocking him back to the ground. Frank didn't have to get any closer to see that his final assailant was dead.

He turned to find the hidden sniper who had pulled his

fat from the fire. Frank kept his pistol drawn but not pointed at the man as he rode from a stand of trees.

"Thanks for the help," Frank said. He holstered his six-shooter when the man slid his rifle back into its sheath at his right knee.

"Damn road agents in these parts ought to be strung up." The man stood in the stirrups and looked at the last man he had shot. "Naw, this is better. I like to see them brought to justice from the muzzle of my gun." He settled back down, lifted his leg up around the saddle horn and leaned forward to better examine who he had rescued.

Frank felt like a bug under a microscope. If there was a single detail the man missed, Frank wasn't sure what it might be.

"Yup, road agents," Frank agreed. "Good thing you came along when you did."

"You riding in that direction?" The man jerked his thumb over his shoulder, toward the south where Clark and his caravan headed.

"Are you?"

"Now, mister, it's not real polite to answer a question with one. Didn't your ma ever tell you that?"

"Are you a lawman?" Frank wasn't able to see the man's chest from the way he was hunched over. A badge might be pinned under his duster or even under his coat and on his vest. The rider sat upright and got his foot back into the stirrup.

"Do I look like a marshal?"

"I can't say you do." Frank took a shot in the dark and asked, "Were you coming this way to join Colonel Clark's company?" He almost repeated the question when the man took so long answering.

"That thought's crossed my mind. Why'd anybody want

such fine country as Colorado to be part of the United States?"

"Those are powerful sentiments," Frank said. He whistled. Barleycorn decided to trot back to see what was going on. A quick grab snared the reins. Frank mounted and got a better look at his savior.

The man wore a tattered brown duster. His coat under it was of better quality and his black vest shone with silver threads woven throughout. A gun belt gleamed from polishing and his boots were buffed to the point he could use them as mirrors when he shaved. Frank wasn't able to see the six-shooter in the man's holster, but he suspected it was a finely wrought killing instrument. Everything about the man spoke of money—and skill. From horseback, he had taken down two men from almost a hundred yards away.

"If you're heading to join with the colonel, why don't we ride in together?"

"You're not already a member of his army?" Frank watched for any twitch or nervous tic that would reveal that the man was lying.

"Can't say that I am. If me and you join together, it's always nice to have someone watching your back. In any army it takes a spell to make a new friend. The ones already enlisted tend to be clannish sons of bitches." The man took his reins and prepared to use the ends on his horse to get moving.

"I'm game," Frank said. "You know where the camp is? I've got a map, but it wasn't marked right."

"Show me."

It took some doing to each hold a side of the map while on horseback, but they turned it around, got their bearings and the man said, "I wasn't told exactly where to go, but this canyon here might be about right. It matches what was said."

"One of the colonel's recruiters told you where their encampment was?"

"Not exactly. Here's your map. It looks like one the army uses."

Frank laughed and added a hint of derision to it.

"The officer wasn't using it anymore." This seemed to satisfy his new partner. They rode together, hunting for landmarks and making small talk. It took a considerable bit of willpower for Frank not to ask too many questions. He got the drift of how the man had learned of Clark's army, and he hadn't exactly been recruited. One of Clark's drunken soldiers spilled his guts about a mountain of gold bars. That was enough to bring this gent down from somewhere to the north. What happened to Clark's soldier never got mentioned. Frank hoped he got a Christian burial.

Or maybe not if he was like the others riding under Colonel Clark's banner. The piles of dead back at the fort were a hint of what was to come. Those on the train, women and children included, were the first and should Clark seize power of the territory, such murderous rampages might only be the start.

Frank never mentioned the wagon tracks he still followed, and his new companion didn't seem to notice. The ruts took off across a meadow toward higher terrain.

"Think that peak's the one you were told about?" Frank asked. One of the Front Range's towering mountains dominated the terrain. A half dozen canyons lead up from the meadowlands into rockier expanses.

"Can't hurt to try. That looks to be a good choice." The man pointed to the middle of three canyon mouths. Frank wondered if he had figured out the source of the tracks cut into the ground or if he was too intent on the high country. He kept his eyes tilted upward, as if hunting for angels and demons ready to swoop down.

They rode into the mouth. For the first time, Frank got cold feet. This was crazy. There wasn't anyone riding with Clark who could identify him, but what was he doing joining the rebel army? If he found the bivouac the smart thing for him was to notify Legende. He had the official connections to deal with the murderous swine, not Frank.

But he wasn't sure yet this was where Clark holed up. The rocky ground no longer took tracks from the cannons and caissons, making Frank wary that he had taken a wrong turn. He needed to be sure so he could lord it over Emily. He and his trail companion rode to the top of a hill and looked down on a broad, grassy mountain meadow. Frank tried to speak but words failed him. He had expected a few ragtag men sitting around tiny cooking fires. Spread throughout the canyon floor was an army numbering at least five hundred. If someone told him a thousand men camped here, he wouldn't put up much argument.

"Reckon we found the right place," his unwanted partner said.

"Reckon you're gonna die if you don't know the password."

Frank Landry looked up into a trio of rifles trained on them from higher in the rocks. He heard movement behind, cutting off any escape. Through dumb luck as much as any skill on his part, he had found the colonel and his army--just a fraction of a second before the colonel and his army discovered him.

❧ 14 ❧

I t is so kind of you to escort me, Paul. I simply didn't want to attend without a gentleman's ... protection." Emily O'Connor smiled winningly. Paul Vandenberg returned the smile with a toothy grin. She saw what ran through his mind as if he had spoken aloud. Oh, how she wanted to play poker with him!

"It is my duty, Emily."

"Duty?" She bristled. "Escorting me is a *duty*?" She faced away and fanned herself. Putting a mirror on the far wall to be able to see his reaction would be a clever thing to do, but she wasn't staying in Denver that long. Traveling had become a way of life for her, hunting out the biggest poker games, sometimes playing in them and other times being paid to deal.

"You misunderstand. It is the duty of any red-blooded man to come to the service of such a fine lady." His compliment rang hollow, but she didn't care. It was something, good enough for her to feign forgiveness.

"Oh, very well. You did kill a man for me."

"That's harsh," he said. "Come along and don't bother yourself with such unpleasant memories." He held out his arm. She looped hers through it, and they walked out to a waiting carriage. The sun had sunk behind the Front Range and a cold wind whipped through Denver. She hoped that was not a foreshadowing of what was to come.

She hadn't gained any significant information about Colonel Clark or the mole on the governor's staff. While Lucius had been removed, she simply could not put together the time line required for Vandenberg to hunt for her and then shoot the former governor's secretary in the back.

If Paul Vandenberg was not a spy for the filibusterer then he certainly knew more than he admitted.

"I get so confused," Emily said. "What's the purpose of tonight's party?"

Vandenberg let out a gusty sigh and said, "The same as all the others. Oh, Governor Routt might proclaim a special day or honor a hero at these parties, but the intent is to raise money for his election campaign once statehood is a fact."

"Do you miss working for Mister Toms? He must be a terribly rich and powerful man." She didn't add that his wife was overly possessive of the man who must be her lover.

"Of course, but working for Governor Routt has benefits. Being in the center of such power is heady."

"Not that you have that much," she prodded. "You're only a hired hand, so to speak. Have you considered running for governor yourself? You know the job and have powerful connections like Horace Toms." She watched the play of emotion on his face, although his features were hidden partially in shadow. The occasional flash of light from gas street lamps turned him into some sort of black and white drawing scribbled in the margins of a book and then animated by flipping through the pages.

"The position of secretary can lead to more powerful posts," he said with a touch of bitterness.

"As it did in Lucius' case?" She saw that Vandenberg was getting angry. "Oh, let's not talk about such things. Who do you think will have the loveliest dress at the ball tonight?"

This forced him into a social mode.

"Why, my darling, you. I don't need to see the other women to know you will be the prettiest there. And your dress is superb. From Boston?"

She rattled on aimlessly about Boston and how lucky women were there to get the latest fashions from Paris, sometimes even before New York. And of course, San Francisco was always months later.

"And, well, Denver," she finished. "It's better than the Hog Butcher to the World, but not by much."

"You are well travelled," he said. "Are you independently wealthy or is there, shall we say, a benefactor financing your roaming about?"

"Why, yes, here we are. And it's about time. I really should have worn a sturdier wrap if I wanted to stay warm, but then that wouldn't be fashionable, would it?" She clung close to him and Vandenberg went into political mode immediately, greeting men already outside to smoke cigars and to talk business.

Emily steered him forward to the door and entered, finally leaving him behind to discuss something about railroad right of way across the southern part of the state. She whirled through the main room, greeting and being greeted and making her presence known. The governor and his wife were nowhere to be seen. Without their acknowledgment, she didn't matter to any of the others in the crowded ballroom. She wasn't a Colorado resident and wasn't going to vote.

This small immunity from notice allowed her to keep a sharp eye out for the Pinkerton agent posing undercover as a waiter. What would interest the Pink would certainly interest her. The entire staff moved through the guests efficiently delivering drinks and hors d'oeuvres. Trying to guess which were also Pinkerton agents kept her occupied. From her reading of them, the way their eyes moved constantly, scanning the room, she picked out three more. The governor had a small army to protect him tonight.

She hoped they were all the agents assigned here tonight. After what happened to her, they might worry something similar would happen to the governor or his wife. Using the woman as a lever to force him to resign or turn over power to Colonel Clark was possible, but such a crude attempt to seize power had little chance of succeeding. Once Colorado became a state, there was no turning away from the laws and constitution that dictated how the new government functioned. If Governor Routt resigned, a line of succession was already in place, dictated by federal laws as well as new state statutes.

That got her to thinking about her attempts to sting Paul Vandenberg into saying something revealing. He was only the governor's new secretary, but if he became lieutenant governor, he would be in line to take over the reins of government. That meant Colorado remained a state without a lengthy process to withdraw, which attempt would be fought tooth and nail back in Washington as well as here in the new state.

Clark's possible seizure of power before statehood became a reality remained the primary threat.

She made her way up the steps to the second floor and glanced down the corridor leading to the suite of offices. Unlike before, no guards were posted. Or were they? She edged down the corridor and pressed her ear to the governor's office door. For a few seconds she heard nothing. Then the sound of someone pacing. She hadn't seen the governor among the revelers below. He might be working while the party danced on. Or the guard had been moved out of sight to set a feeble trap within the office.

Emily sidled away to the next door. She saw a large brass plate with Paul Vandenberg's name on it. He hadn't waited a single second to move into Lucius' office adjoining the governor's. She tentatively twisted the doorknob. Locked. She fished around in her mound of flaming red hair and drew out a long pin. More than once she had used her lock picking skill to break into a saloon owner's office to take money owed her. This lock proved easier to open than many. A sharp metallic click signalled her success. She swung open the door and spun into the room. When she closed the heavy wood door, she leaned back against it. Her heart hammered.

On two different nights she had broken into the governor's office and now his assistant's. The first had gone remarkably well, forcing Routt to guess she was the one who had read his report. The politician freely had shared its contents with her, much to the Pinkerton agent's chagrin. She wasn't sure what she made of Paul Vandenberg's reaction as Routt had related what he knew of Colonel Clark's armed rebellion.

It was time to find documents that indicted Paul Vandenberg or, she was reluctant to admit, exonerated him. Every time she watched emotions play across his face, she read guilt.

Stepping carefully, she went into the room and made a slow turn, taking in the file cabinets, books on a shelf, the desk and furniture. She stood behind the desk and studied it. The center drawer was locked, but from what she had seen of Vandenberg he wasn't likely to keep anything he wanted kept secret in a locked drawer. He was sneakier than that.

"He thinks he's smarter," she said softly. The shelves of books drew her.

More than a hundred volumes were neatly stacked and

arrayed in precise rows. He hadn't had time to move his own books in, if he even considered it. These were all Lucius' possessions. She stepped away and tried to see the entire bookcase as a single entity.

One book looked out of place. It was larger, thicker and not pushed all the way back onto the shelf. It took considerable strength to pry it loose, suggesting that Vandenberg had crammed it onto a shelf already fully stocked with other books. It popped out. A small lock held the cover shut. It took her less time to open it than it had the door into the office.

A hollow cavity cut into the pages held a smaller notebook. She pried it out and held it up for closer examination. Before she had a chance to read even the first page, steady footsteps in the hallway warned her of approaching danger. Hastily stuffing the larger book back into the bookcase, she looked around for a hiding place.

None.

Trying to get out on the balcony would doom her if the doors were locked. And why wouldn't they be after Vandenberg had to know she--or someone--had reached the governor's office that way the night before. No window curtains to conceal her. No space beside a file cabinet. No closet.

Emily dived for the desk and burrowed into the knee hole. Again her heart pounded. She worried it was so loud that whoever had entered would hear.

"Emily?" Footsteps. She held her breath. "Are you here, Emily?" She had her derringer but reaching it amid the folds and yards of cloth in her skirt wasn't possible. She clutched the pin she had used to open the locks. It made a fearsome weapon--once. If she used it, she had to succeed with the first attack.

She imagined going for an eye or the Adam's apple. It was too risky trying to penetrate the heart with a coat, vest and shirt providing layers of protection. She tried to remember if Vandenberg's watch pocket was high or low. The brittle pin driving into a watch case was possible. And that way lay failure to defend herself.

"Are you here somewhere, Emily? I couldn't find you in the ballroom."

The footstep came around the desk. Vandenberg had to spot her if he took even one more step.

"Who's in there?" The sharp question made her jump and bang her head on the bottom of the locked desk drawer. She settled down when Vandenberg answered.

"It's me, Burlington. I was looking for Miss O'Connor."

"You startin' to hide your women in your office, Mister Vandenberg?"

Emily heard a second man enter. The Pinkerton!

"What do you want?" Vandenberg sounded as if he kept his temper only through habit of dealing with more powerful men.

"Security check, that's all. And if it's that redhead you're lookin' for, I seen her downstairs talkin' with Erasmus Higgins."

"Why'd she ever talk to that old fool?"

"Because he owns a dozen hardware stores and is richer than either of us will ever hope to be?"

Vandenberg cursed.

"Go on, Burlington. Make your rounds. I'll see to Miss O'Connor."

"She's one worth seein' to, I'll give you that. You think her and the governor hit it off? He didn't ask any of the right questions about her abduction last night. I think she bewitched him."

"Out, out. Let me lock up." He hesitated, as if thinking. "Let me lock up," he repeated more slowly, as if trying to remember if he had used a key to enter the office. Both men left. Emily heard the sound of a key grating in the lock.

Vandenberg had realized the office door was unlocked when he came in. She clutched the book she had taken from its hiding place and considered what to do. Leaving the way she had come in was risky. If Vandenberg didn't linger outside in the corridor to see if she came out, the Pinkerton agent was on patrol upstairs now.

She heaved a deep breath, wiggled free of the desk and went to the French doors opening onto the balcony. It took her longer than she liked to unlock the doors. Then she was faced with the descent to the ground. It cost her a yard of fabric, but she went to the end of the balcony and shinnied down a drain pipe. Then a different problem faced her. If Vandenberg hunted for her, she had to have an excuse for being outside.

Boldly walking to an older man puffing away on a stogie, she planted herself directly in front of him and asked, "May I join you in a smoke?"

"My dear, why, yes. You smoke? Cigarillos? Cigarettes?"

"Let me try one of those. It's a special Havana, isn't it?" She had no idea but had heard men in saloons boasting how fine the smoke was because the cigars were rolled on a Cuban wench's naked thigh.

"You are very discerning." He drew out an etched silver case and drew out a thick cigar with almost religious reverence. "Allow me to prepare it for you." A quick turn of thumb and penknife cut off the end. He presented it to her as if it were a grand gift rivaling Tiffany's 82-facet yellow Kimberly diamond.

Emily puffed on it when he applied a match and only supreme effort kept her from choking. By the time Paul Vandenberg found her, she had mastered the art of savoring the cigar and had made a new friend with Erasmus Higgins, much to Vandenberg's obvious distaste.

She appreciated this greatly since he barely spoke to her as he drove home with her in his carriage. Emily waved good-night, waited for the carriage to turn the corner, then made her way straight for the Society of Buckhorn and Bison head-quarters so she and Legende could go over the book she had discovered hidden in Paul Vandenberg's office.

E mily O'Connor knocked impatiently on the carved
door. She stepped back and considered shouting for
someone to let her in. It hadn't occurred to her
before that the Society of Buckhorn and Bison was ever
deserted, but she had never seen more than four people in
the huge house at any given time. With Frank Landry out
somewhere finding trouble, only three members possibly
remained. Whatever business he had might take Allister
Legende from the house and Mister Small gave her the
impression of being elsewhere most of the time. He was a big
man with even bigger duties. She just didn't know what they
were.

That left Kingston. A butler ought to tend the home fires.
Why wasn't he rushing to let her in?

Emily started to bang harder on the door when it opened.
Hidden in shadow a figure beckoned her inside.

"It's about time," she said. To her relief Kingston closed
the door behind her. If someone else had answered her call,
she wasn't sure how she would have dealt with the situation.
As much as anything else, she needed an introduction to

everyone who came and went here if she wanted to feel more comfortable with all the cloak and dagger goings on.

"Please wait in the library," Kingston said. "Mister Legende will be down soon. He is dealing with an important message."

"Message?" From high above in the depths of the society's house she heard the frantic clicking of a telegraph key. Unable to read the dots and dashes only made the mystery that much more profound for her. "You have a telegraph line running into the house?"

"Mister Legende is well versed in many things. Would you like something to drink or eat while you wait?" He studied her without seeming to stare. "Or a needle and thread?"

"I have lost a bit of the dress," she admitted. "It was inescapable."

"I am sure it was just the opposite." Kingston smiled and added, "You managed to escape."

"Yes, that."

They went to the library. He opened the door. As she brushed past, he asked, "Would you prefer a cigar? There are some fine Honduran ones in a humidor on the side table. Please open a window, though. The smoke lingers." Kingston sniffed loudly.

"I've had quite enough of them for the evening. A carafe of water would hit the spot, though."

The butler bowed slightly and went off. She had the urge to explore while no one was watching her every move. This house held secrets in every corner. Some of them must be of interest to her.

However curious she was, that exploration had to wait. She went into the library and settled in a chair. The opened the book she'd taken from Lucius' shelf across her lap. Every page held curious groupings of letters and numbers. Nothing made sense as she tried to find a pattern.

"That appears to be a common enough code."

Emily jumped at Legende's comment. She hadn't heard him enter. He poured her a glass of water from a pitcher on the table. She hadn't noticed Kingston leave the water, either, she had been so engrossed in trying to figure out what the code meant.

"Well? Tell me what it says."

"You are growing impatient, Miss O'Connor. Even if we happen upon the key quickly, translating so many pages will be tedious work."

"It must be important. Paul Vandenberg had it on his office bookshelf."

"Indeed. Is there something more about discovering this that you haven't mentioned?"

She explained her reasoning as to how Paul Vandenberg was more likely the one who had placed it on the shelf since it didn't fit easily. Everything about the prior secretary showed how organized he was. Lucius would have hidden the code book, but in the manner of the "Purloined Letter." Somewhere on the shelves of books had to be a few the same height and thickness. He would have placed the book there to blend in.

"So you feel Vandenberg simply stuck it where it was most convenient for him? Yes, that's likely. He is an impatient fellow."

"Have you found out more about his background?" Emily found herself drawn back to the code book and away from whatever Legende had learned. The cryptic cipher had the feeling of urgency to it.

"Quite a lot, actually. He has failed at most things he's tried. Becoming Mrs Toms' lover is the only thing that has given him any success, if you call adultery that. Considering how sexually voracious she is, Vandenberg expended no effort starting the affair."

"There's no question about the two of them?" Even hearing of such scandalous behavior failed to divert her from the code book. "There's a number in the first set of five characters on every page. That must be the key. But how?"

Legende sighed. He took out a pencil and began writing on a sheet of paper.

"The first three numbers show the page number of a book. The next two can be any of several things. Probably the line number and number of words in. Or perhaps it is the count for the word starting at the top."

"So '10392' means page 103, nine lines down and two words over?"

"Or," Legende said, "page 103 and the 92nd word. It will take a little trial and error to read the book."

He flipped through the pages, stopping occasionally to study a drawing.

"If we don't know what book is used as the key, we'll never decode it! How can we begin to guess what Vandenberg would choose?"

"Not Paul Vandenberg. Not the dead man, Lucius, either. Someone is sending coded messages that were recorded in this notebook. If we assume Colonel Clark is the author, what book would he choose? *Moby Dick*? I think not. He isn't a nautical man. Hawthorne or something from the *Federalist Papers*? His actions show little influence of the literary, and trying to prevent Colorado from becoming part of the United States tells me that he isn't likely to go a discussion of our country's founding philosophy." Legende sank back in his chair and closed his eyes.

Emily thought he had gone to sleep, but the eyes popped open and flames seemed to leap forth.

"He thinks he is a military genius. To reinforce that with his subordinates, he would choose a title to impress them."

"Paul Vandenberg is a sloppy man. Even lazy, I would say.

Maybe he stuck the code book next to the one used as the key," Emily said. She gulped at her water. "I don't remember what was next to it. I need to go back and see."

"That is increasingly dangerous for you, and I fear time is running out. The commissioners arrive in a day or two for the local ceremonies prior to signing."

"So soon?"

"It's a preliminary step but will obligate Governor Routt to sign the official statehood declaration within a week of Congressional approval. Whatever Clark intends must be done soon." Legende reached over the table and lifted the book he had been reading. He studied the cover. A small smile danced on his lips as he held it out for her to see.

"I don't read German," she said. "Does Clark?"

"I doubt it." Legende went to the shelves of books and began working his way down one row. He plucked one book from the array. Even before he turned with it, Emily blurted out a cry of triumph.

"That's the book that was next to the code book. What is it?"

"The English translation of *Vom Kriege* used at West Point. While Clark never went to the academy, he certainly has pretensions of graduation." Legende settled back in the chair, took up pencil and paper again and began working steadily. After a minute, he looked up and said, "It refers to page and position of the word."

Emily took another gulp of water and perched behind Legende, looking over his shoulder as he translated the first page. She pointed and exclaimed, "That's his battle plan! What he intends to do to seize power."

"It's quite detailed with complex movements, especially for an army without real training. Even then, he shows his inexperience by not realizing the 'fog of war' is real."

"No plan," Emily said, "lasts beyond the first exchange of gunfire."

Legende looked back over his shoulder at her and smiled. He said, "I knew I made a wise decision inviting you to join the Society." He continued work and finally tossed down the pencil. "These are troop movements, spots to attack and occupy, a complete plan. But we need to know when he will move his army against the Capitol."

"What's that?" Emily tugged at a scrap of paper stuck to the inside back cover. "If he has transferred other messages into the book for future reference, he might not have had time for this one."

"So if it's recent, it might give us something more immediate than a grandiose battle plan." Legende worked down the rows of numbers, flipping through the book and counting to get the translation. He finally turned and looked at Emily. "This is it. He intends to attack in two days, during the ceremony when everyone is paying attention to the dignitaries."

"Wait," Emily said. "That's not right."

"Yes, it is," Legende said, testy. "What mistake did I make?"

"The handwriting is the same as in the book."

"That is true, but ... " Legende's words trailed off. He understood what Emily already had. "This note isn't from Clark, it's to him. The spy on Governor Routt's staff hasn't yet sent it."

"And now he won't since the book and his note are missing. He'll know we found it," Emily said. In exasperation, she said, "Why are we pussyfooting around? Paul Vandenberg is the mole. He shot Lucius, not because he had kidnapped me but because he found I am working for the Society."

"More than that, Vandenberg moved into a key spot on the governor's staff. It makes sense that he is the traitor. But we can't accuse him or have the authorities arrest him without proof. Definite facts, not our guesses."

"He tied me up. He--anybody could have. I was blind-folded or unconscious." Emily sagged. "What are we going to do?"

"Prepare. Can you return the book and note to the office?"

"Won't you need all the details? There must be fifty pages to decode."

"I have basic information and some idea as to strength of his army. It's impressive, but we'll learn more when Frank reports." He chewed on his lower lip in frustration. "And when Mister Small returns. He should have been back by now. I can't imagine what's happened to him."

"Frank can talk himself out of any jam." She said with some scorn, "He certainly talked himself out of our marriage, though it wasn't exactly talk that made me divorce him."

"If past experience is any guide, he will get us what we need," Legende said confidently. "The location of Clark's men, how they are armed, if they have started moving. In the meantime, I will see to heading off argument about post-poning the signing."

"What do you mean? We've found out almost everything. Are you saying the authorities won't listen to you? The governor knows there is a spy in his ranks." She hesitated. "He might think it was only Lucius, but he's suspicious. Tell him what I've found." She held up the code book. "Rather than putting it back since I'm sure Vandenberg is suspicious of me, I'll give it to the governor as proof."

"Getting so much as a note to him will be hard. These are busy times for him, and remember, Vandenberg works as his secretary now. Anything reaching the governor's ear goes through the very man we're accusing of treason."

"You've got the connections. Do something, Allister!"

"I will. I just hope it'll be in time. I wish Mister Small was here since he'll have eyewitness accounts. Or Frank. Where are they?" Legende threw up his hands in resignation. "In the fullness of time, we will find out what's holding them up. In the meantime, Kingston has summoned a carriage to take you back to your hotel."

Emily picked up the code book and made sure the scrap of paper with the time and location for signing the preliminary statehood documents was secured inside. She'd get it to the governor and convince him. Having the madman swoop into Denver with his army would bring too much death and destruction to bear. He had to be stopped before then.

She stepped onto the front porch. The dawn was hours away, and she had plans to make. Emily hesitated at the top step. Something feeling wrong. Across the street a man held the reins of a horse. He moved to keep out of sight. Her fingers closed around the cold metal of her derringer. She started back into the house, then saw the carriage Kingston has called for her rattle and clank up.

Quick steps took her to the carriage. It surged down the street. Emily was sure the shadowy man had mounted and followed her. The two-shot pistol felt comforting in her hand. As much as she could, she found solace in the idea of defending herself from another kidnaping--or worse.

✖ 16 ✖

on't know a password," Frank Landry's riding companion said. "Go on and shoot, if you must, but you'll be passing up two fine recruits for the colonel's army."

Frank was amazed at the man's coolness. The half dozen or more men pointing rifles at them had every intention of firing. He imagined the bullets tearing through his body. He had been shot once or twice, and the pain wasn't something he relished experiencing again. If there wasn't any way to avoid it, he'd go down shooting and try to take as many of the sentries with him as possible. Then, if the others were mad enough, they'd put every single round through him and he'd die quick. No more pain. Over fast. Over.

"Don't reach for your iron," came the whispered order "They're not going to shoot us. Not unless you force their hand."

Frank saw concern on the rider's face, but the concern was about being stupid. He thought he had everything under control, in spite of itchy trigger fingers and nervous guards.

Frank moved his hand away from his six-shooter and sat, trying to look as lazy as a cat snoozing in the warm sunlight.

"You got to give us the password."

"Come on down here where I can reach you, and I'll give you the password all the way up where the sun don't shine. There isn't a password."

"There is so!"

"What is it?" snapped Frank's companion belligerently.

"Auraria forever, that's what it is!"

"Reckon that's right," the man said. "Auraria forever. Now will you let us ride on into camp so we can join up all proper like?"

Several guards huddled together and argued. Finally, one of the waved his hand and called, "Get on down there. Talk to Sergeant Giannini. He's in charge of recruiting and most near everything else."

Frank rode alongside his new friend until they were out of the sentries' earshot. He shook his head in disbelief and said, "Why'd that work? Why aren't we lunch for some hungry buzzard?"

"Because they're not soldiers. Why post so many men unless you want to get them out of your hair? Two guards would have killed us. A half dozen will argue 'til sundown and never figure out what went on."

"*I* don't know what went on, but thank you kindly. You saved my neck. Our necks." Frank rode down the middle of the camp, taking in every detail. One thing bothered him. The army looked big enough to cause real trouble, but nowhere did he see the stolen howitzers or Gatling guns. The camp was spread out enough they might be stashed away elsewhere. That made sense since powder and the boxes of ammunition were dangerous to store with so many cooking fires and men smoking. Without taking a clear inventory, Frank suspected more than a few of the soldiers were already drunk. That and a keg of powder made for a dangerous mix.

Colonel Clark had to be sharp enough to realize his armory had to be separated from the men. This wasn't a real army base with strict discipline.

"The quartermaster's digs." Frank's companion pointed to a large tent with a table in front and a banner flapping above. "That must be the new nation's flag. Right purty, I'd say."

The bright red flag was adorned with crossed gold sabers. A gold lump just above the swords puzzled Frank.

"What's that? The blob?"

"A gold nugget, that's what it is. Auraria is a land of wealth and opportunity for every man brave enough to seize it. You gents come to enlist?"

Frank saw sergeant's stripes and a belligerent attitude. That told him all he needed to know.

"We have," he said. "We were told to ask for Sergeant Giannini. Is that you?"

"Get down from those horses and get your asses over to the table. I can't wait to have two more privates to boss around."

Frank decided Giannini wasn't joking. He had to carry out his charade longer than he expected. If he'd had any sense he would never have ridden straight into the enemy camp, especially with a man with more larceny in his soul than any whiskey peddler or gambler Frank had ever seen. His trail companion strutted over, proud as a peacock, and began filling out forms.

Frank hung back, then led Barleycorn toward a corral. He reluctantly put his horse into the rickety structure, but otherwise he stood out. Trying not to look like a hick tourist in a big town, he began wandering around, catching snippets of conversation. Four men sitting around a campfire drinking coffee that probably smelled better than it tasted, swapped lies about how important they would be once the colonel founded Auraria. One said he'd be a territorial governor while another boasted of being in the cabinet, in charge of inspecting all the women in saloons.

That got a laugh and provoked comments about this being the only way the braggart could get a woman of his own. Frank started to move on when a third one said, "Me, I want to command a company. The home guard. When we take Denver in a couple days, the need for an army ten times this size will be obvious."

"We got that many now," claimed the fourth. "Only the colonel's got the rest of us spread out all around, just waitin' to spring."

Frank settled down and listened hard when the four began discussing tactics. His ears pricked up when one of them said, "I'm kinda nervous, the attack bein' a couple days off."

"Can't be that quick," denied another. "The entire army can't move into Denver and take up positions fast enough."

"We're the cleanup division. You know that. You heard Giannini say so. The artillery and cavalry will take out any resistance in Denver and then we swoop on in and occupy the whole danged city."

"I ought to be with the artillery we stole," said the man wanting to be a cabinet minister.

"It's about there by now. What do you think? Dawn tomorrow?"

This set off a new round of argument. Frank went cold inside. That explained why he hadn't seen any of the weapons stolen from Fort Junction. Somehow he had missed the trail where the cannons and Gatlings were sent on to Denver to prepare for the attack. As early as tomorrow? He had spent enough time in saloons listening to soldiers opining about their superiors. Their captains and majors and colonels were all tyrants and idiots and the forced marches to nowhere always started at dawn. The sentiments and complaints never varied.

Only this time, Frank knew Colonel Clark intended to move fast to stop the declaration of statehood from being signed. He drifted on, leaving the men still debating tactics and times. No one challenged him as he made his way about the camp. The tension throughout reminded him of the way the air felt before a summer thunderstorm in Missouri. He couldn't see it, but he felt it. They were keyed up and ready to explode.

Frank stared at a huge tent with a flagpole outside. The flag was the one he had seen before. The Nation of Auraria had a symbol if not any land to fly over.

He walked past, hoping to get a look inside. The flaps were secured but loud voices from inside told him he had found the heart of the rebellion. Never breaking stride, he rounded the tent, took a quick look to be sure no one saw him, then dived flat on his belly and wiggled closer to the canvas. Gingerly lifting the canvas, he got a look inside.

This had to be the high command for the AoA. He considered gunning down the one wearing the colonel's insignia, then working down in rank. The rebellion ended if he chopped off its head.

But how would he ever get away? There would be chaos and men shouting and shooting at anything that moved, but his chances of escaping were small. He hated to admit it to himself, but he lacked much patriotism or loyalty to Colorado, either as a territory or as a state. More shame was attached to telling Allister Legende that he had failed than letting these madmen blow up the Capitol and prevent the statehood declaration from being signed.

"That'll happen, no matter what," he told himself. Enough people wanted Colorado admitted as the 38th state. If Clark prevented it now, in a month or a year the matter would be resolved. And allowing Clark to remain at the head of a breakaway state was too raw a nerve to endure. The war had settled the matter of secession. Federal troops pouring into the territory to insure statehood would overwhelm any Army of Auraria.

Even if that army used stolen cannons and Gatlings.

Frank scooted a little closer when he heard Clark say, "The heavy artillery is in place by now."

"The officer in charge hasn't reported that, Colonel."

Clark doubled his fingers into fists and leaned forward on a table. The corners of a map blew up as he disturbed it.

"Lieutenant Zamora, send a courier immediately. The howitzers must be prepared to support the cavalry charge. I am not leading the men without proper support." Clark straightened but continued to pin his lieutenant with a fierce gaze. "What of the Gatlings?"

"They'll be in place when you need. They travel lighter. It's their caissons with all the ammunition that are difficult to maneuver."

"Training," Clark muttered. "There should have been training to be sure the men appreciated how to get into formation, move equipment, do--"

"Things move fast, Colonel. You said so." Zamora stood with his arms crossed.

Before Clark exploded, a soldier stuck his head into the tent and called out, "An urgent message for the colonel just arrived."

"Go away," Clark snapped. "Can't you see we are in a strategy meeting?"

"It's from ... from Denver. It's signed Pike. He writ URGENT on the envelope."

"Pike? Why didn't you say so? Bring it here!"

Frank started to slide away, fearing the courier would spot him as he passed the message over. He froze, realizing movement drew unwanted attention. He was better off taking his chances.

"Zamora, the code book. Hurry, man. Pike underscored his name three times. This is highest priority."

The lieutenant passed over a book from a table beside Clark's cot. The colonel worked feverishly to decode the message. He looked up.

"We must attack immediately. The Washington delegation arrives a day early."

"Who is this Pike? How do you know he's not jerking your chain?"

"Do you know who Zebulon Pike was?" Clark faced Zamora. "Do you?"

"He named Pike's Peak. What's that got to do with this Pike?"

"It's a codename for a keen observer. You're hopeless, Lieutenant. Get a cavalry company ready. We attack as soon as possible."

Lieutenant Zamora left, displeased with his commander. Frank backed away and sat up in the dirt, thinking hard. The official signing ceremony was in a few days. But Clark intended to attack right away. He had to get word to Legende and warn him. If the cannons were in place and the Gatlings rolling around but quickly deployed, Clark had plenty for firepower. Now he would add troops to the weapons.

"What are you doin' rootin' 'round in the dirt like some kind of fancy dressed hog?"

Frank looked up at a sentry. The man had a rifle pointed at him. At this range even a poorly trained soldier couldn't miss. Somehow, from the way the man held the rifle, he doubted he was poorly trained. More likely, he had spent his life shooting rabbits and other game. Miss and go hungry. From the considerable girth on display, he never went long without a meal.

"Oh, I was chasing down a set of orders. The wind blew the papers out of my hand. I found them and--" He reached to move his coat away to free his Colt Navy.

"You hold on there a minute, mister." The sentry stepped forward and peered at him nearsightedly. "I know you. By damn, I know you!"

Yeah, sure you do. I'm a soldier just like you." Frank Landry got this feet. The sentry moved even closer, the muzzle of his rifle aimed upward at Frank's head.

"Not that. No, sir, but I know you. You're that whiskey peddler. I seen you in the Oak Bucket scamming Joseph to buy your booze." The sentry shifted the rifle to his left hand and thrust out his right. "Put 'er there, mister. Ole Joseph done cheated me so many times I can't recollect the number. Mostly, he gets me belly heavin' drunk and steals what money I got left. Only, with your whiskey, he can't do that. I never get sick drinkin' it."

"That's a ringing endorsement," Frank said uneasily. "Might be the company can use it in advertising."

"You think that's catchy? 'I never get sick drinkin' it?' Might be worth a sale or two, less you try to sell to the likes of the Oak Bucket. That's what they want to do, make you puke your guts out so they can rob you."

Frank tried to overhear what went on inside the tent. So

much commotion out back was sure to draw Colonel Clark's attention.

"You on patrol back here?"

"Naw, well, not exactly. I roam all around, but I get confused at times. The sergeant said for me to read the signs where I'm s'pposed to walk but, 'tween you and me, I cain't read too good. Oh, good enough, but not that good. The signs make it hard for me, and I don't want to ask too many folks what the signs say. Word gets around."

"You ever go into town?" Frank had a wild idea that might just work. His chances of riding out when he'd just come to camp as a recruit were slim, but someone known to the other soldiers had a better shot of leaving.

"Denver? Sure thing, of course I do. All the boys do, but now we're gettin' ready for the big attack. But you know that, you bein' one of us and all."

Frank put his arm around the man's shoulders and steered him to the side of the tent.

"I have a message, one the colonel wants delivered right away, but I'm needed here in camp."

"I can see that. You with the quartermaster?" The man's eagerness was almost childlike. "You fixin' us up with a wagon of whiskey to celebrate our victory?" He licked his lips in anticipation.

"Shush," Frank said, pressing his finger to his lips. "Don't go ruining the surprise." He fished out a sheet of paper he used to write down orders and began scribbling hurriedly with the stub of a pencil from his vest pocket. "This has to be delivered in town."

"I ... I can't read who it's addressed to. I don't know if I'm the one for this job."

"You are," Frank assured him. "Take this to the postmaster. He'll deliver it to the right place."

"I can do that. I know where the post office is."

"You don't have to say anything, but if you give this to the postmaster, you can say it came from that whiskey peddler."

"You must be some kind of famous if even the postmaster knows you."

"I get a lot of mail from the distillery. Now," Frank said, pulling the man closer and whispering, "You tell him I promised you a bottle, an entire bottle, of my finest whiskey. I've got a special bottle made for Doctor James Crow himself."

"Old Crow?"

Frank nodded. He turned his back to the front flap of the command tent when Lieutenant Zamora pushed through. The man left at a dead run. The courier came next, with Colonel Clark whispering furiously. The courier nodded like a hen pecking corn. Then he headed for the corral.

"Can you deliver the note?" Frank shoved it into the sentry's hand. The man looked at it skeptically, licked his lips and finally shook his head.

"That'd be desertion. The colonel wouldn't like that. Hell, the sergeant wouldn't neither."

"Wait here," Frank said. He lit out after the courier who had saddled his horse and was about to mount. Frank rushed up to him. "You taking the message for the colonel into town?"

"Out of my way. I'm in a hurry." He put one foot in the stirrup. That was all the farther he got. Frank swatted his horse's rump. The animal bucked, then took off at a run. With his foot caught in the stirrup, the courier was dragged along behind.

"Runaway!" Frank shouted. He was glad to see the sentry carrying his message to Augustus Crane reacted fast. With a mighty leap, the man threw his arms around the horse's neck and bulldogged it to the ground. Frank had never seen anything like it in all his born days.

He wasted no time getting to help. When he saw the courier begin to stir, he helped him along to dreamland with a solid kick to the side of his head that put him right out.

"He's in a bad way, Colonel," Frank called. The leader of the rebellion shoved his way through a gathering crowd.

"You," the colonel said, pointing to the sentry. "Take a message into Denver for me."

"Me, sir? Why, yes, sir!" The sentry snapped to attention and tried to salute. He didn't do a good job of either.

The colonel grabbed him by the coat and pulled him to the side. He repeated whatever he had told his original courier until it sank in. The sentry tried to salute again. The colonel ignored it and yelled for Sergeant Giannini.

Frank took the sentry by the elbow and walked him to the corral.

"You deliver my message to the postmaster first."

"But the Colonel said--"

"You'll be in time. Both our messages are real important. But the post office might be closed if you deliver mine after the colonel's and that bottle of Old Crow ... " He let his voice trail away as if the promise of whiskey drained into the thirsty ground, never to be seen again.

"All right, Mister Whiskey Peddler. I can do it!" He mounted, stuck his rifle into the saddle sheath and let out a wild yell as he raked his heels along the horse's flanks. He took off like a Fourth of July skyrocket.

Frank let out breath he had been holding. He had done what he could to alert Legende of the attack. If only there had been more details, but the time of the assault was important. Legende had to know the location. It was time now for more spying. Frank squared his shoulders, tried to look military and marched about as if he was in a hurry to get somewhere. As he walked, he kept a running count of how many troops were camped here and what arms they carried.

All the time he looked for a way out of camp, but he had ridden into a rocky trap. The canyon walls soared so high, climbing them would be difficult, even if he found a trail to the rim. Several canyons branched off. One might lead out but the one he chose to explore was a box canyon. A towering waterfall dropped more than a hundred feet into a pool. From there a river flowed out the mouth of the canyon where he knew at least a half dozen men prevented anyone from sneaking in. He backtracked to explore another of the branches, only to be caught up in a crowd near the corral. He let his horse run free inside the corral as he prowled about to see what the uproar was about.

"Assemble a company now. We haven't much time!" Colonel Clark parted the men like a ship cutting through a frothy ocean. He mounted a horse readied for him by a corporal. Frank watched, wondering what was going on.

"You. Mount up." A strong hand on his shoulder shook him until his teeth rattled.

"Wh-what's happening?" Frank saw the lieutenant who had been with Clark pointing out men all around. They jumped to the corral and readied their mounts.

"The colonel got a special report. We're on the move. Jump to it!"

"The attack? Now? No!" Frank sucked in his breath. It was being launched far sooner than he had said in his note to Legende.

"No questions. And we're not hitting Denver. That's on schedule. This is something else."

"The cannons," he started. The words slipped from Frank's mouth before he had a chance to think.

"That's why the assault will be in two days." Lieutenant Zamora stopped when he realized he was giving away secrets to a lowly private. He turned and glared at Frank.

"Mount up or I'll put a bullet in you here and now. This army has no place for cowards!"

"No, sir," Frank said. "I'm no yellow belly." He vaulted onto the corral fence and whistled for Barleycorn. His horse trotted over. Leaving now with a raiding party led by Clark himself was his only hope of getting away from this rocky prison filled with men itching to spill some blood.

He trotted along in a two-abreast column. The way Zamora watched him sent shivers up his spine. His protestations of not being a shirker hadn't been convincing enough. Unlike his pitch when he sold liquor, he hadn't practiced it and had actually stammered. Planning ahead was easy enough walking into a bustling saloon and selling a product everyone under the roof wanted. Lying to a fanatic intent on preventing Colorado from joining the Union was another matter.

Frank knew he had been lucky not to have been braced by Clark. The report of what he had ordered at the train robbery that financed his entire army rang like a death knell in his head. No quarter. Men, women and children slaughtered. And the memory of the Fort Junction massacre threatened to turn his stomach as he rode alongside the men responsible.

"Column ho!" At the front of the troops the guidon bearer lowered the staff and pointed forward like an old time knight with a lance. Beside him rode the colonel. Frank was only too aware that the lieutenant brought up the rear of the column, an unusual place for such a high-ranking officer.

Zamora prevented anyone from sneaking away from the column--and that included Frank Landry.

They rode hard from the canyon and only slowed when they reached the road heading north toward Fort Junction. Frank's curiosity was eating him alive, but he knew better than to ask questions. The soldier riding beside him was as much in the dark as he was. The only men knowing what had been in the courier's note were at either end of the column, and neither was inclined to give him the answers he wanted.

Miles south of the fort, they cut due east. They set a dangerously fast pace, galloping, then bringing the horses to a walk, a canter and then a gallop again. This wore the animals out slower than a full gallop all the way, giving them some respite but not much. Whatever Clark had been told required a hasty strike. And it wasn't in Denver, unless they were taking the long way around to come at the city from the north.

"Column, halt!" Clark barked the order. He twisted about in the saddle and waved Zamora to the front.

Frank looked for a chance to escape. It would be hard since his horse was exhausted from the rapid pace set for the last few hours, but getting away and alerting Legende made the attempt paramount. Only he lost his chance as Lieutenant Zamora rode past.

"You. With me." Zamora pointed directly at Frank.

The officer waited until he cut away from the column and trotted along behind. Every foot closer to the head of the column made Frank all the more aware of his precarious position.

"We made good time, Lieutenant." Clark snapped his watch shut and tucked it back into a pocket in his olive-drab uniform. "We need scouts posted along the tracks to warn us."

"How long before the train comes?" Zamora watched Frank out of the corner of his eye.

Did the officer suspect Frank was more than a green recruit? If he did, it was folly letting him keep his sidearm. Frank's hand rested on his saddle horn. A move of only inches reached the Colt in his cross-draw holster. He wasn't the quickest with a pistol, but he was as good a shot as they come. Estimates flashed through his head. Take out Clark. Shift to the lieutenant. Then to the corporal hovering so close to his leader.

He tried not to sag when he realized he might hit Clark, but the others were out of the question. He was astride a horse that would rear at the first shot. Worse, the two dozen men in the column were all loyal to their leader. Gunning down Clark signed his own death warrant.

And the way Zamora kept a hawk eye on him insured any gunplay wasn't going to go his way. Getting off the first shot looked impossible.

"The train left Cheyenne on schedule," Clark said. "It ought to come into sight within the next fifteen minutes."

"Cheyenne?" Frank blurted it out before he could check his tongue. "Those're the Cheyenne and Denver tracks?"

Clark ignored him and spoke to the lieutenant.

"Pile debris on the tracks. Stop the locomotive. The delegation will be in a Pullman car, so ignore the first two passenger cars and take everyone in the third prisoner."

"What about the other passengers?" Zamora's question carried a note of anticipation. Frank sat a little straighter when he saw the man's reaction. Clark wasn't the only one with a bloodlust.

"Who cares? Do with them as you please, but only after all the delegation is captured. Ransoming dead men does us no good."

"Yes, sir," Zamora said. He turned to Frank and stabbed a finger at him. "You, get five more men and start blocking the tracks. Rocks, as big as you can move, brush, anything that the engineer will see and brake for."

"Be ready to set fire to the brush, so collect as much as you can," Clark added. "Get on down there, Lieutenant. We have prisoners to take."

"And a nation to build," the lieutenant finished. Both officers laughed.

Frank rode back a few yards and picked out men who looked like slackers. If they failed to build an impressive enough barrier the engineer might plow right on through. That would preserve the lives of untold passengers and get the delegation into Denver safely.

After only a few minutes work on building the barricade, Frank knew that even this feeble ploy of his wasn't going to work. The men proved far too expert at the job, as if they had done it before. If the train tried breaching this blockade, it would derail.

"Good work," Zamora said, inspecting their work. "Get ready. Here comes the train!"

Frank saw the thick clouds of soot rising from the engine's smokestack and knew the carnage was on at hand when Zamora gave the order for them to draw their six-shooters. And on the hill above, Colonel Clark formed his cavalry for a charge that would doom a new state.

❧ 18 ❧

F rancis Marion Landry," he muttered to himself, "you are one colossal fool." He rubbed his hands against his pants legs to clean them of dirt from moving rocks and a sizable hunk of wood across the tracks. Then he had instructed the rebels with him how to stuff dried brush all around until the heap towered more than ten feet high. An engineer seeing that looming on the tracks ahead had to hit the brakes.

It would be better to open the valves, apply full steam and try to bull through it. The risk to the train was greater, but the passengers might live to brag about it. Frank looked around as Clark assembled his small company of soldiers. If they attacked the passengers, nobody would survive. More than one of them already checked the load in his six-shooter or drew a long-bladed knife in preparation of killing.

"Good work, soldier," Clark said. It took Frank a few seconds to realize he was the one being congratulated. He smiled weakly and gave the militia commander a sloppy salute. Clark looked pleased at even this response. Most of the men in his company had no idea how to act as part of a military. They had simply shown up however Clark had recruited them. Word of mouth, the promise of gold and power, whatever it took to bring this woe begotten horde together without any training or pretense of actual military order, had brought them to this point.

The plume of black smoke climbed into the sky, then the locomotive topped a distant rise.

"Set fire to the brush. Now," snapped Clark. "Do it now. The engine takes a considerable distance to stop."

The colonel's aide, Corporal Antrim, tossed a lucifer into the dried weeds. For a second, Frank hoped the fire wouldn't ignite. Then he recoiled, facing away as a wall of heat rushed outward. All the brush had gone up in flames at the same instant. The train's engineer had to be blind to not see that.

"Sparks," yelled Zamora. "Sparks are shooting from the wheels. He's applied the brakes."

"Take your posts. Half on either side of the tracks. Lieutenant." Clark pointed to the far side for Zamora.

Frank was conscripted to join the second-in-command. In spite of his misgivings, he let Barleycorn hop across the tracks and joined the dozen men whispering back and forth. They felt the tension of battle. With this company, that murmur had to be anticipation of butchery.

The train whistle let out a long blast. The engineer applied the brakes even harder, causing the enormous engine to sway from side to side. Frank wondered if it might tip too far and derail. Somehow, the engine remained on the tracks and came toward the now smoldering barricade at a speed where a man riding alongside might jump aboard.

"Wait," Zamora cautioned. "Those of you who were on the other train robbery, you know when to attack. Not yet, not yet ... now!"

The locomotive's cow catcher barely touched the rocks

and other debris still on the tracks when Zamora's squad let out a war whoop and surged forward. Frank cringed as six-shooters discharged. He saw the engineer poke his head up. The frightened man sighted down the barrel of a shotgun held in shaking hands. His final dying act was to jerk back on the double triggers. Both barrels ripped through Zamora's leading men. The ones immediately behind those blown out of the saddle by oo buckshot let loose a curtain of bullets that continued to pockmark the iron side of the cab long after the engineer and coal boy died.

From the far side of the train came Clark's shouted orders, "Stop firing at the cab. The bullets are coming through and hitting us! The passenger car. The third one! Don't let them slip out."

"The hell with that," grumbled a man hanging back as Zamora led his troops toward the rear of the train. "The passengers in the other cars got money. Come on." His wide, crazy eyes passed over Frank as if he wasn't there, but he acted as if he had a companion in crime.

The berserker galloped to the first passenger car and jumped from the saddle to the front platform. Frank tore out after him. By the time he got to the platform, the soldier had pushed his way inside. Gunfire sounded.

Frank climbed the iron steps and swung around to get a good look at the passengers. The only thing that stopped this from being a complete bloodbath was the need to reload. The blood-hungry soldier had burst in, firing wildly. From what Frank saw, two men were dead and a woman had been injured. The killer worked to reload to finish the slaughter he had started.

"Drop the gun," Frank barked. He leveled his Colt and cocked it, knowing what response he'd get. As if he followed the script of a stage play, the action wasn't going to vary one iota.

The gunman spun, six-gun partially loaded. Frank had seen crazy men in his day, men loco from being in the sun too long, men wild from too much booze, men just plain crazy mean. All this gunman wanted was to leave bullet-riddled bodies in his wake.

"You're not killin' 'em. Why ain't you killin' 'em? Shoot, damn your eyes, shoot!" He was incensed Frank hadn't joined in the massacre. He raised his six-shooter and took aim squarely between Frank's eyes. That was the last action he ever took.

Frank's first shot hit him smack in the middle of the chest. He stumbled back, caught himself on one of the seats and looked down at a man cowering on the floor. A feral smile crossed his lips. As if he forgot the man who wounded him, he turned his gun on the passenger.

Frank's second shot hit him in the head, snapping him around. With a dull thud the man fell to the floor.

"Are any of you armed? Take his gun. Reload. Shoot anyone trying to climb aboard."

The man who had almost been murdered unfolded himself from the tight space between seats and picked up the outlaw's fallen six-shooter. A woman from the seat across the aisle began shucking out cartridges from the dead man's gun belt and handed them to the passenger with the gun. Her hand was steady. The newly armed passenger shook like an aspen leaf in a high wind.

Frank backed out to get on his horse when another passenger called, "Mister, you a lawman or something?"

"I ride with the Society of Buckhorn and Bison." Frank almost laughed at the confused expression. He wasn't sure how he would have reacted--and he wasn't sure he understood exactly why he'd said it.

With a leap, he landed astraddle his horse and rode to the second car. More than one gun barrel poked from a window.

He expected to take fire but none of them pulled their triggers. The passengers in this car had things well in hand and defended themselves.

Frank waved as he rode past to the third car, a fancy Pullman outfitted for the dignitaries riding down from Cheyenne. One section of its wall had been blasted into splinters. There were so many bullet holes he couldn't decide if more lead came from inside or out. Zamora had dismounted and fired wildly through the windows. There might have been one pane of window glass still intact but Frank couldn't find it. From the defense of those inside, either the delegation was well armed or they had brought guards with them. It was too much to expect that Legende had telegraphed Cheyenne and set a trap.

If this had been a trap, it was poorly designed and executed. The AoA swarmed all around and cut off any possible escape. Zamora hopped to the platform leading into the Pullman, kicked down the door and emptied his six-gun at the people inside. Frank felt as if he was shooting a helpless man in the back since Zamora wasn't facing him, but Clark's second-in-command played the Grim Reaper for those trapped inside. A carefully aimed shot from Frank's Colt Navy sent Zamora to the Promised Land.

"You shot the lieutenant! What are you, a traitor?" A soldier stared at him from a nearby ditch alongside the tracks.

"He got in the way," Frank said lamely.

"You want to take his place! You'll never be lieutenant. I want to be an officer!"

Frank found himself in no position to argue. The man opened fire on him, ignoring the lead still pouring from inside the passenger car. With a headlong dive, Frank hit the ground, skidded along getting cinders embedded in his elbows and belly. He rolled under the train, protected by one of the steel rails. Wincing with every bullet that *spanged* off the track, he tried to burrow down farther. When he realized he'd never dig himself through the railroad ties, he looked out to see his assailant rushing the train.

It was an easy shot. Frank's first round hit the man in the thigh and brought him down. His second and third went through the crown of the man's hat. His target stopped moving. Mercifully, Frank thought, he didn't have to see what damage his bullet had done to the man's skull. The way his hat became soaked with blood was evidence enough he had brought down another of Clark's kidnappers once and for all.

From his hiding place under the Pullman car, Frank heard the thud of footsteps, the cries, and the never-ending roar of pistols and rifles. Scooting painfully, he shifted to the other side of the tracks, hunting for Colonel Clark. If he cut down Clark down the way he had Zamora, the whole rebellion ended then and there. Peering over the top of the rail, he hunted for Clark. The man was nowhere to be seen. Corporal Antrim held the reins to the colonel's horse, but he was the only one of the AoA killers in sight.

Frank wrestled with the dilemma for only a moment. This was war. He had killed men in his day, and those had been fair fights. He never shot anyone in the back, not until today, until he stopped Lieutenant Zamora from wanton murder. Shooting a man from ambush wasn't something he wanted to make a habit of, but this situation called for different tactics.

And a different morality.

He sighted in on Corporal Antrim. Take him out, deny Clark his horse, give the delegation a chance to escape. His finger drew back. The hammer fell on a spent cartridge. He cocked the Colt again. Same thing. He had gone through the six rounds in the cylinder and needed to reload.

Pinned under the railcar made movement difficult and reloading impossible. He wiggled and flopped from under-

neath and sat cross legged beside the Pullman car to reload.
Frank froze when he heard the metallic click of a pistol being
cocked.

He looked up at the Pullman car's shattered windows.
Colonel Clark leaned half out, his six-shooter held in a steady
hand. The pistol was pointed straight at Frank's head.

"You the only one left? Start rounding up the horses. We
need them for our guests." Clark laughed in a way that froze
Frank's soul.

"I wondered where you'd get horses for them," Frank said
as he stood. The colonel's aim tracked him, then the officer
ducked back into the car. All gunfire had stopped.

Frank winced when a single shot rang out, followed by a
moan that slowly died out. Somebody Clark considered not
worth kidnaping had taken the bullet.

He whistled. Barleycorn came trotting up, whites showing
around his eyes and at first refusing to let his rider mount.
Frank got his seat. He could ride on ahead into Denver. It
wasn't more than fifteen or twenty miles and let Legende
know what had happened. But Clark forced the diplomats
down the steps and out onto the Colorado plains, hands high
above their heads. The colonel had lost more than half his
men, but his raid had succeeded.

How long would it take to get reenforcements into the
field and track Clark to his hideout? Frank knew the route
back to the canyon, but if Clark took his prisoners there, he
had an entire army to defend them. But the cannons and
Gatlings were somewhere else, near Denver, waiting for the
assault on the Capitol. Clark might consider that location
more suitable for his prisoners. What he intended to do with
the delegation wasn't clear to Frank.

Ransom? That hardly worked if what Clark wanted was to
prevent Colorado from joining the Union. Extortion worked
better. Kill the diplomats off one by one and force Governor

Routt to field an army to track him down. That made whatever battle ensued on Clark's terms. Frank had no doubt the
colonel would lose eventually, but a long and bloody fight
served the man as well as victory.

He would have earned a spot in history.

Frank cast a longing glance past the barricade on the
tracks. Ride now and get to Denver for reinforcements? Or
get the horses of those soldiers killed in the battle, let the
diplomats mount and be part of the guard taking them to
wherever Clark intended to imprison them?

Any chance of helping the men escape added to their
longevity. If he wasn't here, he had no way of protecting
them. Frank wasn't sure how he'd do that, but there had to be
something.

He trotted about, snaring reins and leading a half dozen
horses back to the train where Clark harangued the diplomats about the Nation of Auraria. One of the men said something that angered Clark. The colonel whipped out his pistol.

Frank started for him, then saw the other soldiers had
their rifles pointed in his direction. If he so much as touched
the gun in its holster, he was deader than a doornail within
seconds.

"Mount up. Get on those horses now!" Clark pistol
whipped two of the delegation when they moved too slowly.

Once they were on horseback, Clark had Corporal
Antrim string rope from one to the next, a loop dropped over
each man's head. If any horse bolted, they would all die. If
one of the diplomats tried to escape, he would doom his
colleagues.

Clark set his men to guard the column of captives, then
waved for Frank to join him at the head of the column.

"I saw you in the fight. You did good. Ride with me and
tell me what you expect when the Nation is founded."

Frank used every skill he had learned as a salesman to

butter up Clark and appeal to his ego as they rode back to the canyon and the army of rebels camped there. As they trotted through the canyon throat with its half dozen guards, Frank again had the feeling of being the one in the steel jaws of a bear trap.

❧ 19 ❧

Emily O'Connor walked faster. It didn't require a sixth sense to know she was being stalked. The governor's mansion was only a few blocks down the street, but the steady click-click of boot heels behind her warned she had no chance of reaching the front steps where armed guards stood. They were supposedly just decorative and window dressing for the signing ceremonies. "Practicing for the big day," the governor had told her when she asked.

She knew better. Allister Legende didn't need to tell her that the tension oozing from Governor Routt had more to do with the possibility of an armed coup than observance of newly bestowed statehood.

A sudden right turn took her down a street leading to the Society of Buckhorn and Bison. It was closer, but not by much. If she reached the sanctuary it offered, Legende or Mister Small could take care of the man gaining on her from behind. Even Kingston had the air of a man able to deal with problems she could not.

Hurrying, she reached the ornate wrought iron gate. The broad steps to the porch looked so inviting. A dozen paces distant. A sanctuary. All she had to do was knock on the front door. The pounding of footsteps behind her warned that even a few yards down the flagstone path might as well be a mile.

Emily reached into the folds of her skirt, fumbling for the derringer she carried in a small pocket at the same instant a powerful hand clamped on her elbow. She let out a squeal of surprise and tried to break free. Instead, she was spun around and into Paul Vandenberg's embrace.

"My dear, what a coincidence coming across you like this."

"Paul. You're hurting me." She yanked free. He moved to catch her when she lost her balance.

"You're upset. Join me in a cup of coffee. There's a small café not a block from here that Clarissa introduced me to."

"I have a meeting and don't want to be late." She tried to hold her panic down. Out on the street, he wasn't likely to harm her. Or was he? Finding the code book had changed everything. If the governor's new secretary felt trapped or challenged or anything that she did endangered the rebellion, he was capable of anything.

She experienced a momentary lightheadedness when she remembered being kidnapped from the governor's soiree, the crack of a pistol firing, how Vandenberg had shot Lucius in the back, then had to manufacture a blatant lie when the governor himself had come running.

Paul Vandenberg was as dangerous as Colonel Clark himself.

"Going to any meeting in your state wouldn't be proper. A true gentleman simply cannot permit it." He steered her away from the Society's HQ and back toward the Capitol. A hand under her elbow lifted enough to keep her on her toes and off balance. She had played big poker games in both dives and luxurious gambling casinos to know bouncers in both used the same tactics because it worked. The strongest man had to break free. This gave the bouncer a split second to respond, usually with deadly force.

She let Vandenberg direct her toward the café.

"Do you and Clarissa come here often?"

"Often enough when business occupied Horace's time. Now that I am Governor Routt's secretary, I don't have time to while away the hours in idle chitchat."

He swung her around and shoved her into a chair so her back wedged into the corner. The only way she had to get free was to bowl over Vandenberg. The determined expression on his face gave her no hope he would allow that, for even an instant.

"I have a pistol trained on you under the table, Emily. Keep your hands on the table where I can see them. I know you have a derringer hidden away in your skirt."

"My, aren't we being polite?" She did as she was told.

The waiter came over. Emily eyed him, wondering if he and Vandenberg were in cahoots. Even if they weren't, she saw no reason to draw him into the kidnaping. Vandenberg had his gun out and ready. What possible chance did the waiter have?

If the two of them wrestled, she was stuck in such a position that reaching her own pistol would be difficult.

"Tea," Vandenberg ordered. "Earl Grey."

"And a small pastry. I don't care what kind," she said. Emily felt the need to speak and let the waiter know she was present. If gunfire broke out, he might do the heroic thing and come to her aid.

"Of course, ma'am." The waiter noticed her. And why not? She was a lovely woman. As he left, Emily wondered if that had saved him a bullet in the gut. Tangling with Vandenberg would have turned deadly in a flash.

"I suppose you wonder why I brought you here," the man said. He licked his lips nervously and glanced around the café, out the window into the street, and then concentrated completely on her.

"You said it was a delightful place to bring your paramour, I assume the tea is also decent. It's hard to find good tea out on the frontier. Not like in Boston, the Tea Party notwithstanding."

He blinked in surprise.

"Your composure is impressive. It's a shame we are on opposite sides in this matter."

"What matter is that, Paul?" She had won huge pots reading her opponents across a poker table. The slightest hint of hesitation was a signal to act. Her life and possibly the outcome of the rebellion counted on her being exactly right at the precise instant when it mattered.

He reached into his pocket and dropped a slip of paper on the table. Emily glanced at it.

"A coded message? From Colonel Clark?"

"You know it is. You stole the code book. I need it to figure out what Clark's plan is."

"Oh, you know his plan," she said. "I'd guess this says something about his timetable. Are you afraid you'll miss the revolt?"

"I have to know," he said in a harsh whisper. "It's soon. But when?"

"Your tea." The waiter set down two saucers with fine china cups riding in them. A matching teapot was placed on a trivet in the center of the table. "Allow me to pour."

Vandenberg bit his lip at the interruption. Emily looked up at the waiter--the new waiter. He poured her tea, then Vandenberg's.

She reached for her cup, but the waiter lightly touched her wrist.

"My apology, ma'am. Your cup has a chip in the rim. Let me replace it." He snatched the cup from her grip, somehow not spilling a drop and hurried away. Emily watched him vanish into the rear, only to come back with a new cup a few seconds later.

"Where is the book?" Vandenberg drained his tea and put the cup down with a musical clink in the saucer. "I need the book or everything will fall apart."

The waiter put the cup down in front of Emily again. She glanced at it, then looked up and said, "It's the same cup."

Kingston replied, "There's no reason to dirty another." He turned to Paul Vandenberg. The man's eyes had gone wide. His lips fluttered. A dull thud warned he had dropped his gun on the floor. Both hands clutched his throat.

"You poisoned me," he choked out.

"You appear ill, sir. Miss, please help me." Kingston lifted Vandenberg easily and maneuvered him to the backroom. Legende's butler looked significantly at the floor.

Emily picked up Vandenberg's dropped six-shooter and hurried after. Kingston held the rear door open with a foot for her.

She moved through it like a gust of wind. Kingston bent, heaved and hoisted Vandenberg into the rear of a carriage. Then he held out his hand to help Emily up.

"You came at precisely the right time. Now what, Kingston?"

"The Society house is closest." He prodded Vandenberg, who moaned and began weakly thrashing about. "The drug wears off quickly." Kingston snapped the reins. The horse pulled with purpose. In a few minutes, they reached the back of the Society house. Allister Legende stood, arms crossed, watching as Kingston dragged Vandenberg from the carriage.

"It's good to see you again, Allister," Emily said. "I feared that cup of tea might have been my last."

"They serve good tea, but not good enough for it to be

your final cup." Legende held the door open for Kingston to drag Vandenberg in by his heels.

Emily winced as the man's head bounced on every step going into the kitchen, then banged about as Kingston hauled him to yet another room she had never seen. She hesitated to go in, but Legende's hand in the small of her back urged her forward.

The windowless room was bare except for a chair in the center and a table with a large oak box. Emily caught her breath. The chair had leather straps on the arms and legs. Their purpose was obvious even if Kingston hadn't placed Vandenberg in the chair and secured his arms and legs.

Legende walked around and perched on the edge of the table. He drummed his fingers on the box a few times to get Vandenberg's attention. The strapped down man moaned, blinked a few times and looked up.

"I know you. I've seen you and the governor talking."

"Mister Vandenberg, you are about to tell me whatever I want to know." Legende made a sweeping gesture. "Against my architect's protests, I had this room constructed large. He thought a torture chamber should be small, intimate, one where screams were muffled." Legende stood and bent over, his face inches from Vandenberg's. "My philosophy on the matter is different. I want the agony to echo. Let it ring out! If my subject hears his own screams, that adds to the need to cooperate and tell me what I want to know."

Legende straightened and reached over to the table. With precise moves, he opened the box and drew out a wickedly sharp curved steel blade.

"During the Middle Ages, the Inquisitor always did what they called 'showing of the instruments.' Let the subject anticipate what was to come. I prefer sharp blades. This one cuts with no pain whatever. A clean cut is made thusly." Legende swung it. The whistling sound caused Vandenberg to flinch back. The tip left a tiny red stream on his throat. "You won't feel it for a few minutes. Then it burns. While I prefer European expertise in such matters, the Chinese were not unskilled. They came up with the Death of a Thousand Cuts."

Legende swung again. A new streak appeared on Vandenberg's cheek.

"This idea if self explanatory. With such a sharp blade, it is possible to place more than a thousand on a man's torso before the pain becomes overwhelming. You will tell me what I want to know long before then. And, if you don't, eventually you bleed to death." Legende deftly spun the knife around and lightly pinked Vandenberg's other cheek.

"I won't talk! You're the low down, no account rebels!"

"He had a coded message from Clark," Emily said. "If you get me the book, I can find out when Clark intends to attack."

"That's of small interest," Legende said. "I've contacted the Army post in Cheyenne. There are two companies coming down to stamp out Clark's rebellion."

"But they have Gatlings and cannon," Emily protested. "Or has Frank destroyed them?"

"Mister Small has taken care of them. Frank thought to misuse his skills by sending him back as a mere messenger. Instead of wasting effort by telling me what I already knew, Mister Small sabotaged the carriages and caissons. The artillery is stranded out on the plains. They are quite useless to Clark's army."

"What? What are you talking about? You act like you're against Clark. You're working *for* him!" Paul Vandenberg struggled against his secure leather straps.

"Where is Clark bivouacked?" Legende ran his thumb along the blade's sharp edge so Vandenberg could see. "We have our agents in his camp, but they are bottled up, it seems, though one sent a somewhat misleading message to another of our agents."

Behind Vandenberg, Emily mouthed "Frank?"

When Legende nodded, she added, "Gus Crane" and got a second curt nod in response. She sagged in relief. Whatever trouble Frank Landry had found, he was still alive and fighting.

"I don't know! I'm trying to find out. For Governor Routt! I want Colorado to become a state."

"A likely story," Emily said, coming around. She picked through the assortment of knives in the box and held up a rusty scalpel. "Allister, you should take better care of your instruments. This one is terribly rusted."

"I don't clean the blood off that one after I use it. With every new cut, that gives a different ... feel." Legende grinned wolfishly.

"It's true. Everything I said is true. I'm loyal!" Vandenberg heaved, trying to stand. The chair was bolted to the floor.

"If that's true, why do you have the note from Clark?" Emily dangled it in front of his eyes.

"I stole that from Clarissa. She's in cahoots with Clark. Her and Lucius. She was going to kill Horace and take over the railroad. For Clark! And she and Lucius were lovers. I found the code book where he hid it in his office."

"You're saying Lucius kidnapped me?"

"Emily, please! I shot him to keep him from killing you. He wanted to be Clark's right-hand man after the rebellion. You've got to believe me. Ask the governor! He'll tell you."

Emily looked at Legende, then tilted her head to get his attention. She wanted a private conversation. They stepped into the outer corridor and closed the door.

"What he says might be true," she said. "It fits the facts."

"I have had questions about Horace Toms' wife for some time, but I thought she was only a gold digger. If her ambitions were considerably larger, everything Vandenberg said describes a truly cunning woman."

"Queen Clarissa," scoffed Emily. "She and Lucius could have schemed to take out Clark after the rebellion."

"With Lucius dead, Clark wouldn't have to be eliminated. She'd think she could wrap him around her little finger." Legende laughed harshly. "She's underestimated the colonel."

"What do we do with Paul?"

"He's not going anywhere. After the dust has settled, we can learn the truth of his role in all this. He has not played his cards well," Legende said, "but then I always thought he was a trifle naive."

"Too bad," Emily said. "He's handsome enough a brute, but you are right. His skills at intrigue leave much to be desired." Under her breath she added, *Unlike Frank.*

❧ 20 ❧

Frank Landry's frustration built until he wanted to draw his Colt and open fire on anything that moved. Only great resolve held that impulse in check. He rode immediately behind Colonel Clark. A single shot ended the rebellion, but he'd have to shoot the man in the back. Worse, the militiamen who had survived the violent attack on the train all rode behind him. He'd blow Clark from the saddle, maybe even kill him, but all of the would-be soldiers would open fire on him.

One shot, then a volley that would turn him into bloody ribbons. Frank didn't like the odds. Worse yet, what if he failed to kill Clark? Frank didn't want his own sacrifice to be for nothing. He had to be certain Clark was dead.

Complaints from farther down the line of horses told him the delegates were still alive. They slowly recovered from the shock of the attack and seeing so many around their number massacred. By now they must have figured out who had captured them and what he intended. Frank doubted any of the Washington diplomats would die for Colorado statehood.

From their looks, all that threatened most of them was an expanding waistline. They were fat and soft from too many Washington parties and too much wheeling and dealing.

"Just the place for Emily," he grumbled.

"What's that?" Sergeant Giannini spurred his horse to a quicker gait and came alongside.

"Nothing. I was thinking about dinner. It's been too long since I ate."

"I suppose everyone's got a different idea why they joined up."

Frank shook himself when he realized Giannini was a solid Clark follower and threat of death wasn't enough to break his loyalty.

"Yeah, all I want's a full belly. I'd settle for a tent since it looks like rain tonight." He scanned the upper slopes of the Front Range. The scant few puffy white clouds put a lie to his speculation, but he felt the need to explain himself. If he went too far, he'd be gunned down without a second thought.

"Me, I want to see this country stay free. The colonel's a hard man, and I got some complaints about the way he does things, but he can give us all our due."

"What's that? Other than a plate of beans?"

"A homestead. Every non-com gets a section of land over in Middle Park. Heard tell he promised Zamora a governorship down in the southwest corner of Auraria."

"Powerful incentive to obey him, I reckon," Frank said. "What's he going to give grunts like me?"

"You signed on and never asked? He's taken a shine to you. I can tell. Otherwise, you'd be riding at the tail end of the column, eating ever'one's dust. Privates get a thousand dollars in gold and their own horse." Giannini studied Frank's mount. "That horse of yours is a beauty."

Frank patted Barleycorn's neck and said, "And he knows

it, too. Do all the horses get put into the same corral? I'd like to take special care, maybe with a nosebag of oats."

"Ain't got anywhere like that. Or oats. We will, after we drive out the damned Federals."

"That'll be good," Frank said, choosing his words carefully and trying to sound neutral. He swivelled around in the saddle. They entered the throat of the high-walled canyon. He started counting sentries. When he and his unexpected partner had ridden in before, there had been a half dozen lackluster lookouts. Frank counted at least a dozen men, and the way they waved and hollered, they were anything but listless. They knew their leader returned with the key to their victory.

Frank began to sweat as he considered ways of taking away that triumph. Just as he decided to whip out his six-shooter and blaze away at Clark's back, a full squad of men came galloping up from the encampment. They surrounded Clark and escorted him to the command tent. The whole way, the soldiers cheered and waved their rifles around in the air.

"What's to be done with them?" Frank looked back at the disconsolate knot of diplomats. They realized their future was bleak. He wasn't sure what he could do about that, but he had to try something. Soon.

"We got a special place for them. Away down a box canyon leading off the main one, somebody drilled a mine-shaft and stopped within a couple dozen yards. It makes a perfect prison. A single guard outside the mouth can keep the whole lot of 'em penned up," Sergeant Giannini said.

"I'll come along and help out."

"You don't want to grab a mess o' beans? I thought your stomach was grinding away at your spine."

"You said I'd get a thousand in gold. If I keep good watch over them, I'm guaranteed to get it. I don't slack off in my duties, even if I am hungry."

"Gold, yeah," Giannini said. He almost drooled as visions of such wealth flowed through his mind.

Frank started to ask where the colonel cached such a treasure but knew that made him appear too curious. Devoted foot soldiers didn't ask questions, especially ones that sounded like he intended to steal the AoA's gold.

"You bring up the rear. Don't let any of them stray." Sergeant Giannini used the end of a lariat to get the diplomats' horses moving, delivering solid whacks to the rumps of the lead horses. One of the men started to complain and caught the rope across his face. He jerked away as a long red welt disfigured his cheek.

Giannini laughed harshly and pointed. The men, rope nooses still around their necks, began slowly riding down the canyon. Frank let the front of the column round a bend in the rocky trail and rode up to the trailing diplomat.

"I'll get you out. Are you up to it?" Frank studied the man who looked beaten and hardly able to keep his seat. The response heartened him.

"I was born ready. Aren't you with these outlaws?"

"There's no time to explain," Frank said. "I'll see you past the guards at the canyon mouth. Once you're free, head straight back to Denver and tell the postmaster everything. Everything."

"The postmaster?"

"His name's Augustus Crane. Don't argue. I need to be sure the sergeant doesn't torture the others making up your commission." Frank sucked in a deep breath, then pointed toward a crevice leading up to a sandy spit. "Hide up there. I'll be back when it's dark and escort you out. Go. Go!" With a quick move, Frank got the rope from around the diplomat's neck, freeing him.

The man hesitated, then bolted for the narrow trail leading higher along the canyon wall. Frank doubted a way to the top existed, and if it did, Clark had guards posted along the rim. The filibusterer was meticulous in his planning.

Frank put his heels to Barleycorn's flanks and galloped forward to the next man in line, who had already rounded the curve in the trail. He came alongside the man and whispered, "I'll get you out but not now. When it gets dark."

"What happened to Commander Hunnicutt?"

"He's safe, unless you betray him." Frank saw the expression crossing the man's face. He and Hunnicutt weren't friends. They might not even be friendly, but they were in the same predicament. "You need him to help get you safely away."

This convinced the man.

"What should I do?"

"Pretend to escape. I need the guards to think you're the last rider."

The diplomat worked his head free of the rope, let out a rebel yell and jerked at his horse's reins. He shot off the trail and headed for the stream running down the canyon floor. His sudden escape attempt took Frank by surprise, but only for a moment.

"I'll get him." He drew his six-gun and fired into the air. To the fleeing man's credit, he didn't surrender. He bent low and changed direction, as if dodging.

This gave Frank the chance to catch him along the river-bank. The man eyed him suspiciously when he kept his six-shooter out. Frank shrugged and fired again into the air.

"Don't you try that again!" Frank fired again. He motioned for the man to retrace his path back to the trail. The diplomat hesitated, then nodded curtly.

When they reached the dirt path, Giannini and another soldier waited with levelled rifles.

"You do not escape. You will pay for that!" Giannini aimed, but Frank rode between the muzzle and the delegate.

"The colonel wants them all alive. I caught him. He can't get away. He knows it's impossible to escape now." Frank sucked in his breath as he waited for Giannini to take his finger off the trigger. For two quick heartbeats, he worried the sergeant would fire, first taking him out and then the diplomat.

"You're right. Colonel Clark needs them for ransom. All of them."

"In good shape," Frank added. The sergeant wasn't as inclined to agree with him on that point. "Think of how much more gold he's worth in one piece than if he has a slug in him."

Giannini grumbled, then wheeled about and trotted away leaving Frank and the other soldier to escort the prisoner to the mineshaft.

As they neared the mine, Frank perked up. A double-rutted road cut away and ran parallel to the back of the box canyon. At this altitude it took years for vegetation to regrow if it was disturbed, but freshly crushed plants hinted at recent--within days--of a heavy wagon rolling past.

"You and you. Stand guard." Giannini ordered two others into posts higher on the hillside where they could gun down anyone trying to leave the mine. "You come with me. We'll report to the colonel."

Frank felt uneasy at being singled out. The fake escape attempt counted against him. No matter that he had "caught" the prisoner.

The sergeant checked his guards's placement once more, then trotted toward the main encampment, letting Frank set his own pace. Falling behind and simply vanishing entered Frank's head, but he worried that Giannini had other plans. And he was right. Near where he had sent the diplomat into hiding, the soldier halted and half turned in the saddle.

"I do not trust those men on sentry duty. They become

careless and during the fight at the train, they hung back. You rushed in and proved your courage."

"Thanks," Frank said. He pointedly drew his Colt and began reloading. The sergeant made no move showing he disapproved.

"Stay here. Take cover in the rocks. If anyone comes from the mine, shoot them. I'll square it with the colonel if you kill a hostage. And I'll give you a medal if it's either of the son of a bitch guards." Giannini sneered. "I'm not sure he intends for the delegation to be returned alive, but until I know, we must be careful, eh?"

"They won't get past me. Nobody." Frank slid his six-shooter back into his holster.

Giannini grunted and galloped away, leaving Frank alone on the trail. He kept alive by being wary. He clambered onto a large boulder and watched the sergeant's dust cloud move steadily toward the rebel militia camp. Trusting Frank to do as ordered was the sergeant's biggest mistake. Sure a trap wasn't laid for him, Frank climbed down and walked to the crevice leading to where the escaped diplomat should be hiding.

He stopped when something felt wrong. Or maybe he heard movement above him. He looked up but did not draw. The man he'd cut from the column of prisoners towered above him, a heavy rock hoisted above his head.

"Come on down. We're going to make what the Denver newspapers will call a daring escape." Frank waited for the man to look around, then lower the rock and slip down the far side. In a minute the man came toward Frank, leading his horse.

"What're we going to do?"

"First of all, we find a change of clothing for you." Frank considered returning to the mine and cutting down the guards. It wouldn't be hard since they thought he was one of them, but what did he do then? With ten escapees, leaving Colonel Clark behind became far more difficult. He decided to play out the hand with only one of the delegation not being held for ransom.

"Stay behind me, head down. Here." Frank ripped at the sleeve of the man's expensive coat. There wasn't much he could do but dirty the vest and trousers. The shiny black ribbon down the outsides of the pants stood out like a watch fire in a camp filled with men recruited from the Denver slums and worse.

"This suit of clothes cost more than you've likely seen in a month of Sundays," the man said with disdain. Then he laughed and began smearing dirt on his pants and otherwise trying to camouflage himself.

"I'll buy you a new set of duds when we get out," Frank said.

"No, sir, I'll buy *you* the best to be had in Denver."

"That's a deal," Frank said. He mounted and rode at a canter. Time crushed in on him from all directions. Getting the man he'd saved from Clark's clutches was an important part of staying alive. But more than his own neck, he had to save the nine remaining diplomats and keep Clark from preventing Colorado's statehood. Frank was certain Clark wouldn't succeed but in the long run deaths could tally into the hundreds or even thousands. Such slaughter had to be avoided.

"Nobody's looking at me," the man said.

"You're Hunnicutt, right?" Frank grinned at the man's shock at knowing his name. "You're famous."

"But I'm only ... " His voice trailed off as a squad marched toward them, the drill sergeant barking out cadence. The soldiers somehow managed for each and everyone to be out of step. Frank wasn't sure how they did that, but it meant an easier fight if they were pitted against US Army troopers. No discipline, no coordination.

Frank held up his hand so the man wouldn't budge. With more confidence than he felt, Frank ducked into the first tent. A man snored loudly on one bunk. The other was empty. Frank began rummaging through saddlebags thrust under the cot, trying to make as little noise as possible. He dragged out a shirt and pants, then silently backed from the tent with his prize.

"Around back. Here. Change."

"What if they don't fit?" The man patted his rotund belly showing he spent more time behind a desk than drilling or even riding. "I understand. Make them fit." Hunnicutt stepped behind the tent, leaving Frank to stew. Every rider passing by, every soldier on his way across the camp, every eye in the entire bivouac watched. He knew it. Frank jumped a foot when Hunnicutt laid a hand on his shoulder.

"No need to be skittish, son. You either get us out or you don't. I won't be any worse off if you fail."

"That's some philosophy you've got there," Frank said.

"I was in the war and faced many a Rebel rifle. I came through without a nick." He shook his head ruefully. "I did catch typhus that almost did me in, but no Johnny Reb ever scratched my hide. I'm tough."

Frank didn't want to get into a pedigree matching contest. He was a Southerner but hadn't fought and could never support slaveholding. But politics aside, like his namesake Francis Marion, he was proud of being from South Carolina.

Hunnicutt looked strange in the poorly fitting clothes, but not so much that he drew attention. Frank led the way through the camp and rode directly for the narrow canyon throat and the freedom it promised.

"You remember what I said?"

"Go to the Denver postmaster and tell him everything."

"Even before you go to the authorities. Chances are, if you tell Crane what's happened to you, the authorities will know by the time you reach them."

"So, quite the efficient intelligence network, eh? I assume you and this Crane are on the proper side?"

"I don't have to be on the podium at the statehood ceremony to support it," Frank said. He clucked his tongue to stifle any reply. They came up to the nearest guard.

The man picked up his rifle and sauntered out to give Frank and Hunnicutt a once over.

"Where you headin'?"

"The colonel's sending a courier with an important order." Frank inclined his head in Hunnicutt's direction.

"What's the order?"

"It's about the Gatling guns and their deployment," Frank said. "Any more 'n that's nothing you need to know." He made a big show of taking out his pocket watch and checking the time. To Hunnicutt he said, "You're going to have to gallop the whole way to get Colonel Clark's orders out in time."

He saw that the guard was impressed.

Frank fixed a cold stare on the rifleman.

"Well? If he doesn't head out right now, we'll have to report back to the colonel."

"Get to riding," the sentry said. "Like your horse's tail's on fire." He laughed and swatted the rear of Hunnicutt's horse as the diplomat snapped the reins and started toward Denver.

Frank kept the guard engaged in small talk until Hunnicutt disappeared. This was the only sentry who had to be fooled. The others up in the rocks watched but saw no reason to respond.

He considered riding after the delegate, but there were nine others being held prisoner he had to save. How he'd do that was a poser. He bid the guard goodbye, turned Barleycorn's face to ride back to the encampment, then drew rein. His mouth went dry.

Frank stared down the barrel of a rifle.

"You got plenty of explaining to do," Sergeant Giannini said. "And I hate traitors so much, I hope you can't talk your way out of this because I want to put you in front of a firing squad."

21

A firing squad is too good for you," Sergeant Giannini
snarled. "I'm going to cut you down here and now."
He pulled the rifle stock firmly into his shoulder.
Frank saw the man's finger tightening on the trigger.

A dozen ways to escape raced through Frank's mind.
Nothing was good enough to avoid getting blown out of the
saddle. He started to go for his Colt Navy since talking his
way out of this wasn't possible.

"Hey, Sarge, don't. Don't shoot. I got a better idea."

Both Giannini and Frank looked back toward the militia
camp. A rider had come up unnoticed, his six-gun firmly in
his fist. Frank silently thanked the man he had ridden into
camp with for staying his execution, if only for a few seconds.

"What're you saying? He helped one of them get away."

"I know he did. That's water under the bridge, but do you
think Colonel Clark is going to notice there's one man shy?"

"So what?"

The rider positioned himself about halfway between Giannini and his squirming target. Frank still couldn't hope to draw
and fire before the sergeant took him out. The man who had

joined him on the ride back from the Fort Junction massacre had rescued him once before when they rode into the canyon. Frank worried that deliverance wasn't at hand a second time.

"He's going to shoot the lot of them, isn't he?"

"You don't know that," Giannini snapped. His ire turned toward the man delivering the news. "I heard he was, but you don't know that."

"It's a better than even bet he'll get mad if he doesn't have the proper number of criminals to execute," the rider said. "One rode out, but you know that. Who's the colonel going to blame for that?"

"What are you saying?" Giannini looked panicked now that the import settled in. He had been in command and Clark wasn't a forgiving man when it came to such failure.

"Take this one and pen him up with the delegation. All Clark wants to see are ten men lined up and shot. Do you think he'll check the identity of every one of them?"

"You're saying I should put this one with the others and fool the colonel?" Giannini turned thoughtful now as the terror slipped away.

"It's all a matter of him getting what he wants. Nine men shot. No good. Ten? He's pleased as punch that his sergeant is on the alert, and that ought to be good enough."

"Are you sure he's ordered them all executed?" Giannini lowered the rifle.

Frank started for his Colt, only to have the rider reach over and pluck it from his holster first. The man whispered, "Go along with it and we'll all get out of this alive."

Frank had no choice. He raised his hands to show surrender.

"I should report to the colonel," Giannini said. "Take him to the mineshaft and double the guard on the prisoners." The sergeant glared at Frank. For an instant he looked angry enough to go ahead and shoot. Instead, he jerked at his reins and trotted off.

Frank let out a breath he hadn't realized he had been holding. He studied his savior--his two-time savior. Or was he actually rescued this time?

"I never got your name."

"Call me Buster. And we're not out of the woods yet." He scanned the rims of the canyon. He silently counted the guards Clark had posted.

"I saw eight sentries," Frank said.

"There're at least fifteen. He's expecting an attack. That's why he's going to shoot his hostages." Buster used Frank's six-shooter as a pointer. He saw how Frank watched and added, "I'd better not give you your piece back. Giannini might not see but word travels fast in this camp."

"Did Clark order the murders?"

"Of course he did. He never intended to ransom the diplomats. Why should he? There's a mountain of gold back there. He's a rich man, if he just sneaks off with what he's already stolen. That's not what drives him."

"He believes in what he's doing," Frank said. He had come to this conclusion early on.

"Clark's failed at everything else he's done," Buster said with a touch of bitterness. "He wasn't an officer. Maybe he wasn't even a soldier. The only thing we can be certain of is that he's one hell of a snake oil salesman."

"How do you know about him?"

"They call me Buster because I'm so damned good at breaking broncos. Bronco buster. Get it?"

"What? That's no answer. I--" Frank shut up when he saw they were within earshot of a squad lugging crates of ammunition toward the mouth of the canyon. He needed to guard his tongue. As he rode, he glanced aside at Buster. The man was on his side and might even be another agent recruited by Allister Legende.

"Faster," Buster said. He spurred his horse forward. Frank raced to keep up. If Giannini saw the prisoner trailing the captor, he'd start asking the wrong questions.

As he rode alongside Buster, he asked, "Are you a member? Of the Society?"

"I was a Mason once upon a time. Got bored." He bent low over his horse and raced along the trail to the mine.

"Not what I meant," Frank called. Then he saw that the time for jawing was past. A full squad of men preceded them and lined up at the mouth of the mine.

Colonel Clark hadn't wasted time sending the firing squad.

Buster saw them and yelled, "Wait! Don't start without us!" He cast a quick glance at Frank.

Frank touched his empty holster. His ally rode closer and passed over the pistol. Even with two guns blazing, they faced a dozen men with rifles. Frank was a good shot but taking out six men with his first cylinder wasn't all that likely.

"You come to help us? The colonel didn't say anything about that." The corporal in charge looked up and smiled. "Hey, it's two of us what helped capture them back at the train."

"Antrim, isn't it?" Buster rode over to the corporal. "Why aren't you back in camp helping the colonel? Without you, he'll get mired down something fierce."

The corporal swelled with pride at being recognized for his role in the revolt. Frank saw the others milling about without direction. Antrim hadn't given the orders yet for the massacre to start.

"Pleased to have you join us," the corporal said. He turned back toward the mine where the diplomats were penned up. As he did, Buster jumped from the saddle like he was bulldogging a calf. They went down in a tangle, giving Frank the chance to act.

He whipped out his Colt and pointed it at the squad.

"Drop those rifles!" His words carried the bark of command. Half the militiamen did as he ordered. Three looked confused. Only two responded by taking aim at Frank. His six-shooter barked out leaden death. Five shots, two dead. He swung his gun around to cover the rest. "Drop the rifles!"

His repeated command produced results in the only soldier who hadn't obeyed. The man started to shoot Frank. A final slug ripped straight and true.

"Run! Retreat!" Frank's next command sent the surviving men scrambling for their horses. Frank needed those horses for the delegates to escape. He dry-fired, cursed, then slid to the ground. With a quick move, he scooped up a fallen rifle, knelt and began firing.

His aim was disturbed when Antrim and Buster crashed into him. With a swift move, he slammed the rifle butt into Antrim's skull. The corporal went out like a light. Buster panted, recovered and saw the fleeing squad.

"That was mighty dumb, chasing them off like that. They'll bring reinforcements."

"I had to get rid of them. We were outnumbered." Frank emptied his rifle, cast it aside and picked up another. They had plenty of firepower, but their targets galloped off. Only three horses remained where the firing squad had tethered their mounts. That was nowhere near enough transportation to get all the captives out of camp.

Frank left Buster to gather the rifles. He reloaded as he went to the mineshaft and yelled, "Come on out. If you want to get away, move it!"

The bedraggled men filtered from the mine. Some

shielded their eyes against the sun after the darkness of their rocky prison. But several pushed forward.

"You were one of them. So was he!"

"Catch." Buster tossed the man a rifle. "If you can't use it, give it to someone who can."

"I served with General Grant in four major campaigns. I know how to shoot."

"Get to higher ground," Frank said. "We're going to have to keep alive for a while."

"You have reinforcements on the way?" The man's muttonchops rippled as he ground his teeth together. "As I feared. We're on our own."

"With carbines," Frank said. "Search the bodies. Take whatever weapons you can find." To his relief, three of the men hurried to obey. He stepped back to survey the terrain.

"There're plenty of spots giving cover," Buster said. "Get the men with rifles up high to hold the road leading back to the camp."

"Lack of ammo is a problem," Frank said. "Instead of making a stand here, let's try to get out of this box."

"By now the rebels have reached camp and told somebody what happened. Clark can either let us rot here or wipe us out." Buster thought hard. "He'll send as many troops as he can find. He doesn't want us hitting him from the rear."

"He's that close to launching his attack on Denver?" Frank worked over everything. Too much went on about which he knew nothing. This wasn't the fog of war. This was the absolute midnight, blinding blizzard of war.

"I'll do what I can to divert his attention." Buster thrust a rifle into Frank's hands. "You've done good so far. Keep it up." He turned his horse, mounted and let out a loud cry as he rocketed off.

Frank started to yell for Buster to return. When two of the diplomats came to stand beside him, he changed to,

"Good luck." He looked at the older men. From their expressions, battle wasn't unknown to them. Either knew more about troop movement, positioning snipers and actual combat than he did. But they looked to him for leadership.

"Spread out," he ordered. "Stay clear of the mine. Don't get boxed in. If you get a chance head up the canyon walls and get the hell away from here. The main canyon's open at both ends but I don't doubt that Clark has a squad guarding each."

"Not much ammunition," said the man on his right. "If we follow your partner out of here, we stand a better chance. Attack, son, attack. Defense never won a fight."

"Take cover," Frank insisted. "Make every shot count. Our chance at getting past that many soldiers is close to zero." He worried that Buster had slipped past at least a company of militia marching toward them. A quick hand pushed down one of the delegate's rifles as he raised to fire. Frank repeated, "Every shot has to count. Even if you're a sniper, these carbines aren't much good at this range."

"I am good enough," the man said, "and you're right. This isn't the proper weapon."

"Take cover and get ready," Frank said, looking around. He hoped the colonel had cached weapons and ammunition in this constricted space, but he saw nothing but the road leading toward the south off the main track. The deep ruts made him want to investigate, but he suspected gold lay at the end of that road, not anything to keep him and the statehood delegation alive.

A quick check showed the men had chosen well. He believed it when some said they had military training. That might save the lot of them when lead started flying. No panic, just carefully aimed return fire.

He told himself that when the first ounce of lead unexpectedly tore though the air a foot over his head. He flinched, ducked and dived for cover.

By the time he situated himself behind a rock, there wasn't a square foot of space anywhere not buzzing with bullets seeking to rob him of his life. Frank waited until the first attack began to fade. Their attackers had to reload or clear jams in their rifles. He popped up like a prairie dog, looked around, then opened fire. The lead element in Clark's company was less than twenty yards distant. Frank's skill proved itself immediately. He shot the legs out from under the soldier.

"Good shooting, son!" The gray-haired man who seemed to be the leader of the delegation chanced a peek around the rock where he had taken shelter. He got off a few rounds. Frank wasn't able to see if any rebel had caught a bullet because a second wave broke over his head.

White gunsmoke filled the air with a choking fog. Frank's eyes watered and his heart hammered. When he checked his rifle's magazine, a curious calm settled on him. He had only two rounds left. A pair of measured shots emptied his carbine. He slid his Colt from the cross-draw holster and waited for the attackers to break through. At point-blank range, he could take out a few more.

Then it would be over.

"Listen!" The gray-haired man shouted at him. "Do you hear that?"

The tenor of the attack changed. Fewer bullets came their way. A sudden breeze cleared the smoke from a patch immediately in front of them. The militiamen fired toward their rear. Frank got off a couple shots and winged a rifleman. Then a miracle happened. The rebels began surrendering.

Frank wasted no time in yelling, "Throw down your rifles and grab some sky! Do it!" He boldly stepped out from behind the rock, now almost chipped away from the barrage that had been directed at him. "Into the mine. Give up. Surrender!"

"Don't shoot. We're not gonna let ourselves get massacred." A soldier wearing sergeant's stripes shouted at the men in his company still fighting to quit. When they saw they weren't going to be killed if they gave up, the remnants of the fighters threw down their guns.

Frank herded them into the mine where the delegates had been held captive.

"Sauce for the goose, sauce for the gander," the gray-haired diplomat said with glee. He issued orders to several of the others in his delegation with rifles to stand guard. The way they obeyed without question showed the chain of command in the delegation had been restored. That done, he hoisted the rifle to his right shoulder in proper Army marching style and said to Frank, "Let's greet our rescuers."

It took Frank a second to realize what had happened. He hadn't forced the surrender. Other than the bullets in his six-shooter, he was out of ammo. So were the others around him. Two had been hit and one killed--and no one had so much as a single cartridge left. They ran a big bluff to keep the cowed rebels imprisoned.

"That's what happens when fake soldiers clash with real ones," Frank said. Blue wool jackets and bright brass buttons gleamed in the sun as the US cavalry advanced. "You'd better greet them, sir," he said to the diplomat in charge. "I might be mistaken for a rebel."

"So you might, so you might." The man chuckled. "They don't know you freed us, you and your partner coming in before they lined us up and executed us. That was bold, son, mighty bold." He slapped Frank on the back, then greeted the captain in charge of the rescue party.

Frank heaved a sigh of relief. Either his note to Augustus Crane sent by illiterate courier or the diplomat he had sneaked out of the camp--someone!--had brought the troops riding in when it mattered most. Either way, his action had saved the day by letting Legende know where Clark's men were camped.

The rebellion was over before it really began.

Frank slid his Colt into his holster, then was knocked backward as a bullet whined in his direction.

❧ 22 ❧

Frank Landry fought to sit up, but the weight pressing him down was too great. He tried rolling to the side but was thwarted at this, too.

"Stop fighting me. Lie still." The voice came from far away. The roar in Frank's ears faded, and he shook his head to get at least one clear thought back.

"Legende? Why'd you tackle me?"

"Sniper. It's got to be Clark." Allister Legende pushed away from Frank and remained flat on the ground. He pulled a fur-lined canvas bag up alongside and worked to unlace the side.

"What is that?" Frank jumped as a bullet smashed into the ground an inch from his head. He strained to see where the shots came from. The nearest place was more than five hundred yards away on a hilltop.

"Now!" Legende yelled. "Take cover." He took his own advice and let Frank trail him behind a rock so nicked from the previous gunfight that the side facing the militia encampment was scoured white. Tiny stone chips piled up beneath the face.

Frank moved faster once he decided any of those bullets could have ended his life. Then another almost did. A sharp pain shot through his side, driving him forward. He scrambled about and pressed his back against the rock. He lifted his left arm. Blood soaked through his vest and coat.

"You're all right," Legende said, not being at all gentle as he pulled Frank's left arm out straight from his shoulder. "The bullet went between your chest and arm."

"Both are bleeding," Frank protested.

"Sissy." Legende opened the flap on the canvas bag and pulled out a Sharps .50. Working methodically he slid in the magazine tube with the shells, adjusted the sights for elevation and only then did he twist about and rest the rifle in the crook of his left arm, sighting in on the distant hill.

"That's Clark doing the shooting? He's come close to snuffing me out a couple times. That's powerful good shooting."

"Yeah, it is," Legende said. He took in a deep breath and let it gust out like a train's steam whistle. He drew back on the trigger. The powerful recoil half lifted him off the ground. He levered another round into the chamber. Frank expected him to fire again right away. Instead, he bided his time.

This was a waiting game between the two snipers. At this distance, the slug arrived long before the report from the rifle. It was an invisible death stalking them. Frank quickly corrected that.

It was an invisible death stalking Colonel Clark, too.

Legende fired again. He controlled his breathing and waited until Frank wanted to scream out for him to shoot. When Legende pulled the trigger again, Frank yelped in surprise. He saw how the round was discharged, yet it seemed that something had gone wrong and that Legende had shot himself.

"Damnation, the man is good," Legende said. Blood

spurted from a head wound. He whipped off his bandana and pressed it into the wound so it would clot over faster. "What are you waiting for?"

"What do you mean? You want me to doctor you? I've had some experience but--"

"Clark, man. Go get Clark. I hit him. I don't think I killed him, though. The feel was wrong." Legende rested his Sharps against the rock and used both hands to fasten the cloth around his head. He had lost his hat somewhere. By the time he knotted the bandana he looked like the illustration Frank had seen in a book about sea-going pirates. All Legende needed was an eyepatch to match an illustration on the cover of a dime novel.

Frank reached for the rifle, only to have Legende shove him back.

"I need something with more range than this." Frank patted his Colt.

"No one uses Natty but me."

"Natty?"

Legende scowled. "Natty Bumppo. That's what I named the rifle. Now get after him. We haven't come this far to let Clark slip through our fingers."

Frank took a quick look over the rock, then dared to expose himself. No silent slug hit him again. He hunted around until he found a rifle someone had dropped. He checked its magazine, then started hiking for the hilltop where Clark had taken the shots at him. As he climbed to the crest, his left arm and side gave him considerable pain, reminding him he might be walking into a trap. Then he picked up the pace. Clark had plenty of opportunity to take him down reaching this point. Frank hoped Legende kept a sharp lookout and would use "Natty" if the chance presented itself.

A few yards shy of the hilltop, he levered in a round and

crouched low. He took a deep sniff of the air. A gunpowder stench lingered. Hearing nothing but the wind picking up as it gusted down from higher elevations, he cautiously advanced. A rifle lay in pieces on the ground. Frank knelt and examined the weapon. One of Legende's .50 caliber slugs had torn its way along the length of the barrel, destroying the stock and blowing off a fancy telescopic sight.

"He did wing you," Frank said, running his fingers over the stock. They came away smeared in blood.

From this vantage point the only escape lay down the hill. Clark headed north. At least his fang had been pulled. The long-range rifle was destroyed as a killing machine.

Frank wasn't the best at tracking, but as Clark fled he made no effort to hide his trail. He plowed straight downhill. Frank lit out after him, reached an arroyo and found drops of blood on a rock to guide him in the proper direction. Stride long and every sense straining, he rounded a bend in the dry stream bed. He brought his rifle up to cover Clark.

"You betrayed me," Clark said through gritted teeth. He pressed his right hand into his side. Blood seeped around his fingers. "Worse, you betrayed the cause. Auraria's flag should fly over this proud land, not that of the damnable Federals."

"People across the territory want to join the Union," Frank said. Warily, he approached. "They voted. You wanted to set yourself up as ruler by killing anybody who disagreed with you."

"You're a pawn." Clark fixed his gaze on Frank. "I never heard your name. What is it?"

"Frank Landry, not that it'll be any use to you. You'll be locked up in the Laramie Territory Prison. But not for long. I've heard they have a gallows there and work it around the clock."

"A Federal prison," Clark said. "I don't think so, Mister

Landry." He pulled his hand away from his wound. A four-barreled pepper box discharged all four slugs simultaneously.

Clark recoiled when the gun blew up in his hand. And Frank's reactions were up to the task. He pulled the rifle trigger the instant he saw Colonel Clark make his move. The round from the Winchester snapped Clark back against the arroyo bank. The colonel looked down at his burned hand, then reached for the new bullet hole in the middle of his chest.

Frank stood frozen to the spot. He'd killed the man responsible for so much death and destruction. And it ended so fast. So fast to die.

He retraced his steps. He had to report back to Allister Legende and find what to do next. He had no idea since he'd never been in a situation like this before. Somehow, he knew this wouldn't be the last time.

Frank Landry smoothed wrinkles from his coat and adjusted his new vest. With a quick look at his pocket watch to be certain he arrived exactly on the tick of six o'clock, he knocked on the door. Kingston was equally prompt answering.

"Good evening, sir. Mister Legende is pleased that you could join us." Kingston stepped back, holding the door. Frank entered the foyer. The Society of Buckhorn and Bison was as imposing as ever, but now he heard laughter and the tinkling of glasses coming from the council room. Kingston silently led the way and stood by the door, bowing slightly to grant Frank official entry.

The others had already arrived. Frank restrained the impulse to look at the engraved invitation in his coat pocket. He was certain it read SIX P.M.

"Well, well, well. Mister Landry has chosen to grace us with his presence." Emily O'Connor lifted a glass sloshing with red wine.

"It said six," Frank muttered lamely.

"Better an hour early than five minutes late," she said.

"Oh, never mind. Have a drink. Allister has opened his marvelous wine cellar. This is a truly superb wine, Allister. Congratulations on your splendid taste."

"Would you prefer whiskey, sir?" Kingston stood at Frank's elbow, holding a silver serving tray. A glass of amber whiskey rested on a white doily.

"This is more to my taste." Frank sipped it, considered the taste for a moment and lifted his glass in Legende's direction in approval.

"Only the best for members of the Society," Legende said. "Please be seated. Kingston wants to begin service."

Frank found himself seated across from Emily. Her emerald eyes glowed, reminding him of so many times when they were married and something amused her. The easy, lilting laugh and the toss of her head, the way her red hair caught the light and turned into a golden crown—

He took a longer drink. Those days were over and the divorce had been finalized years back. They had both travelled to Fargo to complete the legalities of separation since a small legal industry had built up there for such things. It had been businesslike and swift. She had left, heading west, and he took a riverboat north up the Red River to Winnipeg.

Frank started to ask her if she regretted it, then drained his whiskey. This was not the time or place for such discussion. And, looking back on their lives, she had no reason to ever lament scribbling her name at the bottom of the separation papers.

Frank looked around the table. Mister Small sat at the far end, opposite Legende. The man's size dwarfed the china service. He almost daintily sipped at his water. The crystal goblet vanished in his huge paw. Other places around the table had been set but no sign of the intended occupants was to be had.

"I see you noticed the empty chairs, Mister Landry."

Legende got to his feet. "One is for Augustus Crane, who is unable to attend our banquet because of other pressing business." He saluted the chair to his left. Kingston silently moved the chair and placed it against the wall.

"Why doesn't Kingston take a seat and let the others on the staff serve?" Emily shifted in her chair and raised a toast to the butler. "His participation equals our own."

"It is difficult to both serve and be served, Miss O'Connor." The butler bowed slightly in acknowledgment of her compliment. He moved to the other empty chair and waited silently.

"Then there are those who have left our ranks." Legende nodded. Kingston moved the chair and placed it beside Augustus Crane's.

Legende went to the mantle, removed one of the bullets standing sentinel there and tucked it into a vest pocket.

"Wait," Frank spoke up. "Who's missing? Was he part of our mission? Is Buster one of the Society?"

Legende's expression never changed. He returned to his chair and sat, the leader presiding over his troops.

"I don't know anyone named Buster."

"He might have given me a fake name. He saved me a couple times and--"

"Begin service, Kingston," Legende ordered, ignoring Frank entirely. "I am sure our guests have worked up an appetite after all that they've been through."

"Some of us, at least," Frank said, seeing that questions about Buster fell on deaf ears. Moving his left arm still gave him the twinges.

"Mister Small has overseen the return of the Army's stolen weapons and ammunition. Fort Junction is once again fully staffed and an active post. To your success, Mister Small." Legende toasted the giant. For the first time, Frank saw a smile on the huge man's lips. He lifted his glass, too, thinking to only make the gesture. Whiskey almost spilled onto the table. Kingston had refilled it without being seen.

"And to you, Mister Landry. You successfully defended the kidnapped delegation. The preliminary ceremony, strictly for the local politicians and press, went smoothly. Governor Routt and his staff are now on the way to Washington for the formal statehood ceremony with President Grant. Colorado will become the Union's 38th state."

"To the Centennial state!" Frank was surprised that he and Emily voiced the same toast at the precise instant. At least they weren't finishing each other's sentences.

"It was my pleasure to be the one responsible," Frank said. He smiled broadly at Emily, "when others flitted about going to fancy dress balls and eating dinky hors d'oeuvres while making small talk." With feigned effort, he lifted his left arm to the table and turned slightly to show where Colonel Clark's bullet had almost robbed him of his life.

"Miss O'Connor is too modest to relate her own role," Legende said. "Let me say it was consequential. She exposed Mrs. Toms' role in the plot. Without her giving Clark the train schedules and the combination to the safe, the gold financing the rebellion would never have been stolen. And Miss O'Connor implicated the governor's former secretary, Lucius."

"Don't forget that I exonerated Paul Vandenberg. He was such a bumbling fool playing spy the way he did. He could have hanged for treason." Emily beamed in self-admiration.

"I heard tell that he's been replaced." Frank sought some small defeat for her.

"Governor Routt graciously took my advice on that point, yes," Emily said. "Paul has been reassigned to some minor functionary's job where he won't get involved in political intrigues."

Before Frank could retort, Legende cut in. "I congratulate

you all for your part in this successful undertaking. Miss O'Connor, if you accept full membership in the Society, your previous debt will be forgiven."

Frank perked up at that. Legende had recruited Emily because she owed him money. That explained her presence tonight. She was otherwise likely to have taken the first train out of Denver. She didn't like staying in one town too long, especially after a big, winning poker game.

"And Mister Landry, you, also, are invited to join the Society as a full member. All that we discussed as your payment is approved."

Frank looked around the council room. The Society showed taste and elegance in all it did. He suspected that was due, in large part or even entirely, to Allister Legende's management.

"Will I have to work with her in the future?" Frank pinned Emily with his stare. She looked amused at his concern.

"There may be times requiring such cooperation. All Society members are cordial to one another." The way Legende said it was an order rather than an observation. "However, many of our assignments demand the lone wolf approach which you are so well versed in, sir."

Frank sat back and let Kingston serve the first course. Each new course challenged Frank's ability to guess what it was until he was completely stumped by the dessert. He jumped a foot when Kingston ignited the mound of cake and ice cream. Clear blue flames licked the side of the confection. As the butler made his way around the table, setting fire to everyone's dessert, Frank took the opportunity to ask a question that had been gnawing at him for some time.

"Legende," he said, not pretending to be on a first name basis with him the way Emily did, "I have a question that you've ignored."

Legende raised one eyebrow and made a gesture urging Frank to ask.

"What happened to the gold Clark stole?"

Legende laughed and said, "That wasn't the question I thought you were going to ask. Well, Mister Landry, how do you think the Society pays for all this?" He made an expansive sweep of his arm, encompassing the people, the table, the entire mansion that served as headquarters.

Frank has suspected something like that, but he didn't want to appear mercenary in Emily's eyes. She had accused him of being too much of a money grubber when they were married just as he believed her to be a spendthrift

"What question did you think I was going to ask?"

"The answer is baked Alaska, invented by chef Antoine in New Orleans." Allister Legende held up a spoonful of the flaming dessert until the fire died, then he popped the ice cream and cake combination into his mouth with obvious gusto.

Frank Landry joined him. Like everything else about Allister Legende and the Society of Buckhorn and Bison, it was first rate.

The End

Front Range Rebellion

ABOUT THE AUTHOR

Brody Weatherford is a crusty old rapscallion with dozens of blood-churning Western pulps to his credit published under a host of trail-blazing pen names. He lives somewhere west of the 100th meridian in a spacious log home with three dogs, ten cats, and a palomino named McGee.

STAGE COACH AMBUSH

A triple boom and splintering wood trim exploded across Emily's view.

"I don't think so," Frank said.

Emily gripped the little Colt .41 she carried beneath her skirt when she traveled.

More return fire and Frank urged her to stay down.

"Put away your silly little pea-shooter."

"It's not like you're doing us any good," Emily hissed. "You only have two shots left."

"It's not like I have a steady hand." As if to punctuate the remark, the coach bucked high into the air and came down with a crash.

Emily stomped her foot against the floorboards. He was right, of course.

Frank being right was a habit she resented.

"If they would only come closer, I could get a clear shot. If only..." But Frank's words were lost in a hideous squeal from the left rear wheel as Finnegan cranked the horses sideway with a violence Emily couldn't have imagined.

She fell sideways, thudding into the wall as the coach

almost turned over before righting itself with a bone-jarring crash.

Frank too hit the sidewall with a thump, then fell back in his seat, stunned, his revolver loose in hand.

Get The Guns of Legende #2:
Death Waits at Yellowstone

LOOKING FOR OTHER WESTERNS TO KEEP YOU UP AT NIGHT AROUND THE CAMPFIRE?

Try The Punished, a dark western trilogy from
Western Fictioneer Lifetime Achievement Award winner:
Jackson Lowry

Undead
Navajo Witches
Bayou Voodo

LOOKING FOR MORE THRILLING WESTERN ADVENTURE?

BLOOD-CHURNING TALES CULLED FROM THE FINEST OF THE SIX-GUN JUSTICE PATREON REWARD STORIES BY THE BEST OF TODAY'S WESTERN YARN SPINNERS.

CLICK HERE TO GET YOUR COPY ONLINE!

Made in the USA
Monee, IL
03 July 2022

99028085R10134